HARROW

by AMANDA TROYER

Copyright © 2014 by Amanda Troyer
Cover image © 2014 by Amanda Troyer
Cover design by Amanda Troyer
First edition, 2014

Published in the United States by Ivory Deer Books
Printed in the United States
Ivory Deer Books
www.ivorydeer.com

ISBN-10: 1-942035-01-2
ISBN-13: 978-1-942035-01-5
Summary: When Brenna Bowman is plagued by hallucinations, she finds that her already horrible life can get much worse, and has to save herself from murderous visions.

Cover title font is Nail Scratch by Misprinted Type
Cover name font is Garogier by Rogier van Dalen

CHAPTER ONE

DUST SWIRLS AROUND in cursive when I kick tiny pebbles across the parking lot. Potholes litter the less used portion of the blacktop, and I hang back waiting for a lull in customer activity. Through the wall of clean windows I watch a few people dart around the modest convenient store, grabbing staples and alcohol, before heading home for dinner. Frank Allen is working the register, letting his son stock the shelves because his kid has been useless at small talk lately; missing his cue for "Did you find everything okay?", and always forgetting the "Have a great day."

I haven't seen Mabel all day.

Grass at the edge of the lot rustles, inches from my feet. Something flashes in the corner of my eye, and I jump back when I see a black snake swim into the high grass. I shake out my hands that I've tangled anxiously at my mouth while waiting. My nails, jagged from chewing them so much, catch on my shirt when I straighten it. I have to get a job. I have to get myself out of this town. Eventually.

The bell above the door rings when I walk in. As soon as he sees me his face turns somber and apologetic. He doesn't like Mabel, not too many people do, but I'm not my sister. My hands move automatically to my side-swept waves of dark brown hair, and I wring them, spinning it all into one bulky spiral across my shoulder, then swallow hard. "Mr. Allen?"

It's a good enough start; last time I didn't make it through the door.

"Brenna?" His face softens a bit, as much as a hard-lined farm boy face can soften, but his eyes give away his apprehension.

"I saw your hiring sign and I was wondering..." I pause to stand straighter, but in turn let my gaze fall to the floor. "I can do it. I'm a fast learner."

"Brenna, where's Mabel today?" There's a little Kentucky twang in his voice. It reminds me of my dad.

"She's not here, I swear. She'd never know I work here. I avoid her, but..." I start to say I can't help it, that she is what she is and I can't control where she ends up, but I know that's not going to help me any. She's my sister and I can't escape her.

"But?" Frank knows. He knew when I walked into the store, and he let me embarrass myself asking anyway. His hands on the counter's edge hold him steady as his eyes bore through me, watching with pity and condescension. His son looks just like him. Square jaw, overhanging brow, and ears slightly too small for his face.

"I swear Mr. Allen. I'm a hard worker."

"And your sister is a troublemaker. I can't have that here."

As my mind runs through the best excuses for my sister's actions, I run my tongue along my teeth and feel grit from too many days without brushing—too many days spent avoiding home all day and crashing once I sneak inside. I swallow hard again.

"Plus, there's your dad," He says this a little softer, like it's some secret. A can hits the floor, a deafeningly loud sound in the silence that follows Mr. Allen's comment, and we whip our heads in the direction of the noise. His son gapes, wide eyed, caught eavesdropping. He's close to the floor, in an awkward squat, stocking a low shelf. Marcus knows my situation. It's not like we haven't been in the same schools since kindergarten. There are only a few dozen kids per grade. He moves out of sight after muttering something, an apology maybe. Something inside of me dies. What started as a fiery ambition is now a shovel full of charred wood pieces tossed aside, burned and useless. I nod vigorously, forcing a smile, before ducking back out the door into the summer's sticky, hot air. My face is already burning, and not from the invisible heat streaming from the sky, though those sting my cheek bones as well.

The sun doesn't take a break in the summer, beating and burning my scalp as I walk miles around town aimlessly. Hannigan, Kentucky—settled sometime after Lexington, and not too far from said city—is a giant pile of shit. It's large enough to have more than one school, but only one library, three liquor stores and only one doctor. We're a convenient stop on a large highway, so we have more gas stations than any other stores combined. Plus, a handful of chain restaurants close to the exit ramps. I walk past a McDonald's and wish I had a dollar, or two. I'm hungry.

It's early afternoon and I can't take the empty feeling any longer, so I start checking pay phone coin catches and the cracks in the sidewalk for change. Three quarters, a dime, and nine pennies. The faded yellow arches cast a shadow in my path, and I turn around hoping for more change on the way. I duck, narrowly missing being scalped by the bottom of a highway sign. Watching my feet when I walk is getting dangerous. I hit the jackpot at the curb under the money window of the burger chain and have a grand total of three dollars and fourteen cents. A swish and thud from above sends a jolt of surprise through my hunched spine and, before I can catch myself, I fall sideways onto the edge of the curb.

"We can't serve you unless you got a car," A blonde girl says, hanging out the window at me. She chews her gum like a cow chews grass, and the wet smacking sound echoes in my ears.

"I know," I say, with the least amount of offense I can

manage. I use my arm to shield myself from the glaring light of the sun, but her face is still mostly shadows above me. "I just found some change. I'm coming in."

She pats her hand on the wall above my head, and I flinch at the sound of skin on bricks. "Kay, just not through the drive through, alright? Gotta get a car."

I decide not to state, again, that I had no plans to walk through the drive through, and take my handful of change inside to buy lunch.

I eat alone—unless I count the employees I hear laughing from a break room, but they aren't eating. They're laughing. I sneak a peek over my shoulder to see if I can figure out what's so funny, but I don't see anyone at the counter.

I could fill out an application for this, or any of the other corporate chains that have visible signage from the highway— I've thought about it a million times. But when I go to write my name I can't put pencil to paper; I just see the kids from school behind the counter, laughing together. Avoiding me. I can't completely blame it on Mabel, but I do anyway. At least at Mr. Allen's Shop-mart I'd only have Marcus avoiding me.

It's three point eight miles from the highway to my street, two point one is where "downtown" starts and three point three where the sidewalks end. One half of a mile is broken pavement crossed periodically by dirt alley roads. I never want to stay home, so I find myself counting steps to nowhere.

I take First Street and pass the Police station on the corner. Two squad cars are parked in the lot, meaning two are out patrolling. One is likely following my sister. Not that they'd ever catch her doing anything illegal.

The buildings are old, but not unkempt, until you get to my street anyway. Across the street is Randy's bar, then you get an eyeful of crap in the windows of Tater's goods—the town's constant yard sale. A few old row houses on the street drip rust from their metal shutters before you hit the clinic and a gas station. I drag my hands along the broken bricks of a decorative half wall lining the sidewalk, feeling the sharp texture change in depth as I pass each square. With my eyes focused on the ground, I accidentally catch a sharp nail edge, scraping the palm of my hand. The cut is nearly the entire length of my palm.

"Shit," I curse at my bleeding hand while it pools a thick red. I tip my wrist and watch the liquid drip onto the concrete by my shoes, then wonder how vampires could possibly drain people bloodless. Who could hold that much fluid in their stomach? A strange mosaic forms on the sidewalk as I picture an attractive dark figure sucking my life force out through my palm. I snap out of my head when my hand starts to sting. I don't know how long I was daydreaming, but it had to have been a while because I'm feeling light headed.

The clinic is empty. There are only two cars in the lot, and they belong to Dr. Don and Becky. Last year, Dr. Don fixed me up when I tripped over a concrete parking bumper, scraping my arm bloody on exposed re-bar. I didn't have to pay then, I hope I won't have to now. I push through the door, into the waiting area, and instantly feel dirty. The floors reflect my face and ammonia fumes choke the air. I drip blood onto my foggy reflection.

"Brenna?" I snap my gaze from the shiny floor to the middle-aged woman behind the reception desk. Her big curly perm is branded into my brain from as far back as I can recall memories. Becky grew up with my mom and never lets me forget it—we keep it all in the family around here.

"So, I cut myself." I show my hand and a drop of blood falls from my elbow, splattering on the pristine surface below. Blackness creeps into the edge of my vision, far away where I can't reach it to push it back.

I suck in a breath. "Did you know I usually faint at the sight of blood?" Becky nods, running to my side, and steers me into a chair behind the desk as she runs off down the hall. I assume she's getting a rag, or bandage, or something.

"Hey there, little one." Dr. Don calls most kids little one. It doesn't matter that I'm nearly as tall as him at five foot five. He drags me to the sink in the first room, and sticks my hand under cold running water making me wince.

"How long did it take you to get here? You let this bleed a lot." We watch the red swirl with the water as it goes down the drain. "When you get cut you need to stop the bleeding, so next time find a paper towel or something."

"I was outside." I peer out the window above the exam table, and catch two guys walking across the lot. "There's a nail in the bricks and I didn't see it."

"Good thing you got that tetanus shot a year ago." He wipes my palm with a paper towel and peels back the skin to see how deep it is. I cringe, but it's not so horrible that I can't bear it. He looks like he belongs in a medical tent, in some war torn country. His hands are huge, and he's sturdy like an army doctor, I assume, would be.

"It's not bad," He closes my hand around the paper towel. "Want stitches or some glue?"

My stomach turns at the thought of thread being sewn into my flesh, "Glue."

Dr. Don smears a roller ball pen of solution across my cut, and blows on my hand a few times before showing me his work, "Look, all better."

His smile is contagious. It's the first time I think I've smiled all day. But those feelings rarely last long.

"Hey Brenna?" Becky calls me, and I walk into the hallway between her and Dr. Don, rubbing at the weird plastic holding my skin together.

"Don't pick at it," he whispers, nudging me into the waiting area where I come face-to-face with two large, country boys. They both have pointy boots, and jeans, and I can't help envisioning them flying off the back of a cow—they seem like the type.

"Honey, have you seen your sister?" Becky asks as she rummages around the counter for something.

"Sister?" The one wearing a baseball hat arches an eyebrow at his new knowledge. I don't like the hollow feeling I get from seeing his face.

"I can tell her you were looking for her, if I ever see her." I turn to leave, but they follow.

"Here, let me get that for you." Baseball hat guy grabs the door, all gentleman-like, and he's close enough I smell his cologne, with it's overly musky odor. I can't get outside fast enough. When someone is looking for Mabel it isn't ever a good sign.

"How about you take us to her." He's so close behind me I have to close my eyes to ward off the claustrophobic feelings. His shadow engulfs me in hostility. I don't turn around. "I haven't seen her in two days."

A few steps away, the blonde side-kick obnoxiously clears his throat.

I mistakenly walk away from the windows, and angry hat-man yanks me by the arm to face him. "Liar." He slams me up against the clinic wall by my neck, and squeezes hard enough that I can't pull in air.

The other guy clears his throat again, and his voice is a strained whisper, "Danny, let her go,"

"Shut up, Nate."

Danny barely gives me enough oxygen to stay conscious, and my vision starts to fade, "I swear to God, I don't know."

"Don't lie to me, girl." And in an instant it's like I'm at home, taking all the blame for Mabel, taking all the beatings. The trouble she starts always finishes through me, in the form of black eyes and bruises.

"Is there a problem over here?" A faint voice calls from across the lot and Danny drops me. His muscular arm towers above my head as he pivots to face the visitor, like we're all good friends just hanging out.

"Officer." Nate chokes on the word.

"We were just having a chat, no problems." Danny looks at me expectantly, and his smile is smeared with hatred.

"Just talking," I say. Not that I couldn't say he was bothering me. Officer Millard would tell them to leave me alone, but then I'd have yet another reason for this creep to want me skinned. And, considering I don't know what he wants, I need all the favor I can get. Not turning him in may be the difference between a broken arm, and a muddy ditch.

"I think you boys should be running along." Millard says, his hand resting on the handle of his gun, and his long nose tilting upward as he peers down at them. He's trying really hard no to look so young. Danny goes for my arm to take me with him, but I slip it out of his grasp. His mouth contorts into a smirk. I hold his gaze, and start debating the possibility of living inside the police station.

"Later, Brenna." My name on his lips sends my skin crawling. Tears pool in my eyes as I hug myself and slide down the wall. I have to leave this town.

"Come on, sweetie." Millard takes my arm and guides me to the sidewalk. We walk, his arm around my shoulder, toward the gas station, watching the two men drive off in their elevated pick-up truck.

"I'm okay, really." I try to side step his grasp, but he gives me a little squeeze.

"You don't have to be so brave." His polyester uniform is scratchy on my bare shoulders. Even though it's meant to be comforting, his hug feels suffocating instead. He lets go to open the glass door to the store. Inside, he walks to the counter for cigarettes, "Grab a snack or a drink, I'll get it."

It's a nice gesture but I'm not entirely sure it's heartfelt. His stance, as he flips through a tabloid on the counter, is cocky, as if he thinks his nasty habit happened to conveniently save my life. I browse the shelves, and scan the coolers, stopping to pick out a large bottle of juice. I can take it home and make it last a few days.

The door to the bathroom opens when I pass and I'm breathless.

"Hey, Sis." Mabel doesn't seem fazed, only flips her blonde hair over her shoulder. I thought bleached blonde hair would make her look strange, clashing with our olive-skin tones, but it always works so well on her.

She takes my hand in hers, "What ya got there?"

"Strawberry-mango."

"Here." She pulls a wad of bills out of her bra, and hands me a five. I quickly stuff it in my pocket before Millard sees it. She raises an eyebrow, but only shrugs at my odd behavior.

I take the juice to the counter, and let the officer pay as he makes small talk with Mabel.

"Having a good summer?" he asks.

"The best." She smiles with an annoyingly cute head tilt.

"How's your dad doing?"

Neither of us answer.

"Well." He grabs his pack. "Stay out of trouble girls." Then he tips his hat, like some sort of old west sheriff, and leaves.

"That's impossible." I glare at Mabel as she stands wide-eyed shaking her head.

"What do you want me to say?"

"I want to know what the hell you've gotten into. Why are there two body-building cowboys ready to strangle me, just because I'm your sister?"

She purses her lips, and rolls her eyes. "I doubt they were going to actually hurt you."

I grab her by the neck and smash her up against the door as hard as I can—as hard as he did—making the bell jingle, but she shoves me off just as quick.

"Stop!" she screams. "I get it!"

"I don't think you do."

"Take it outside." A hairy attendant, from behind the rows of scratch off tickets, whines at us. He has an unbuttoned polo shirt on, letting his chest hair balloon toward his chin.

Mabel brushes off her ruffled shirt, and crosses her arms over her chest as she follows me out the door. "Brenna, I think I've got something good this time. Real good."

"I don't even care." Humid air mixed with gasoline fumes leaves me light headed.

"You will," she snaps.

"Just leave me alone!" I say, shaking my juice bottle at her like a lunatic.

She takes it and chugs the pink liquid, and I know it's childish but I hit the bottom of the bottle anyway—her shirt is ruffles and polka dots.

"Bitch!" She drops the juice and it spills onto the pavement at our feet. I'm a little angry for losing my refreshment, but the way she pulls at her shirt in horror is well worth it. Her loose silver bangle falls from her wrist, and I snatch it up, holding it from her like ransom. She should buy me a new drink.

"God, Brenna." Her shoulders slump, and she's lost the excitement in her eyes. "Just trust me about this one, okay?"

I grit my teeth, and shake my head. Lies, always lies.

Her face drains of color as she looks past me, and I'm willing my heart to keep beating even though I'm not filling my lungs with air. I finally let out the breath I'm holding when she takes off running around the gas station into the tree line. My neck muscles strain as I whip my head around to look for what Mabel is fleeing from. The jacked up truck rumbles down the street, and all I can think is: run.

CHAPTER TWO

WHEN I SEE their truck driving toward the gas station, I panic. I take off running and don't look back. They don't even see Mabel somehow. I end up crawling behind the hedges at the long abandoned Catholic Church at the edge of town. One the whole town says is haunted.

"Brenna..." Danny sing-songs my name, and I can't help the sick feeling in my gut that says this time I won't be as lucky as the last. Their heavy boots crush twigs and dried leaves, a dozen yards from where I'm crouched, as branches dig painfully into my skin. I don't dare breathe. They circle back, checking behind bushes at the edge of the church property, careful not to leave an inch unsearched.

"Come on, girly," Nate calls for me, pleading in fake desperation. "We won't hurt you. We just want what your sister stole."

Like that isn't something I've heard my entire life. 'Come

here, I won't hurt you' is almost always followed by, 'You shouldn't have done that' or 'you forced me to'. I never walk away from that phrase without pain.

Danny is still wearing the hat, that I'm sure is to hide his receding hairline, and looks ready to explode. His body is tan and toned, but his hair is out of his control. Just like me. He takes the red hat and crushes the brim in his giant hands wringing, and wringing, until a tear forms at the edge. He notices, and throws it to the ground.

"We're going to find you, you little bitch, and when we do…" He pauses and smirks. "It's not like anyone will give a shit that you're missing."

It doesn't hurt as much as he'd like it to. I know no one would miss me, but I don't really feel like committing suicide about it just yet. They start yelling at each other but they have walked far enough away now that I can't understand all of what they say. While stealing glances back at the two men I feel along the stone wall in dappled light until I hit a sharp edge. There's an alcove that holds a tiny stained glass window, but when I push it doesn't move. Sneaking inside a possibly haunted church isn't my first choice, but considering how fast they run, it looks like my best option. The row of bushes end at the next window, and I watch the men argue for a quick second before I crawl forward as lightly as possible.

Mulch scrapes my knees, and shins, and sticks to my hands, but I can't stop. I check them again as I reach the window, and they're watching the hedges in my direction. They can't possibly see me though, I can barely see them. I look at my dirty fingers and realize the thick silver bracelet is reflecting the little pockets of light. My heart stops as they start a slow saunter toward me. Their faces are smug but there is a certain level of murder in their eyes too. I frantically kick behind me at the window, at least if I break it I'll just be bloody and safe, not bloody and dead.

"I told you we'd find you." Danny squats down, and I kick again behind me, feeling like a donkey but I don't care. I cry out when he grabs at my wrist but the kick opened the window. I shove hard off the trunk of the shrub, and slide through the awning.

My feet hit the floor, followed by my butt, and my back, before I hit my head against a wooden barrel. The window slams shut, I hear it click like a lock as the two men try desperately to open it. Not that they could squeeze through if they manage to get it unstuck. I sit up on my hands and they aren't just covered in mulch, but some kind of basement slime too. I'm really glad I chose glue instead of stitches. I stand and brush them off on my shirt, but I can't tell if it's helping. It's too dark. All the light shining in from the three multi-colored windows ends, abruptly in mid-air, two feet into the room. Darkness drew its territory line, and the light isn't permitted to cross it.

The men wedge themselves into the bushes to kick at the window, but it's immobile material. Their feet don't even shake it. I can tell they're tired of fighting with it, and it's only a matter of time before they find another way in. I turn around, feeling into the darkness with outstretched arms. The slime on the floor slows my steps, and the smell is finally settling in my nose: rusting rotten wood, and warm beer. The barrels must have some kind of wine or ale that spilled at some point. The room is large, or I have bad depth perception, because it takes forever to get to a wall. When I finally do it takes even longer to find the stairs. Half a flight up, I hit a metal door and run my hands along it until I get to the knob.

Of course the door creaks. It's not like being in a church in complete darkness isn't creepy enough. The door has to creak too. A long, amazingly loud creak that wakes the dead. It's a good thing there isn't a cemetery for miles. I shut the door behind me, and take in the tranquil stale air of the hallway. The church has been abandoned for as long as I can remember, and there are rumors about it being haunted, but Dad said it was to keep riff-raff out while the land-owner neglects the property. I don't want to believe in ghosts, gods, or devils, so I straighten my shoulders. I walk with my head high, all while my heart races, anxious to get out the door. Everything is painfully tight inside my chest, blood slowing on its way in and out of my heart.

It's not as dark in the hallway, but the cold wisps of air chilling my spine almost make it worse. The windows are boarded up. Though, tiny splinters of light sneak in anyway. The carved wooden doors are heavy with layers of dirt and dust, but also just heavy in general. I heave open the first one I come to, and scurry inside before it crushes me when it closes again. The sanctuary is much brighter, with harsh shadows from the mid-day sun shining inside. I walk into a beam of light and slowly take in the massiveness of the room. The ceiling goes up three stories and curves toward the center in elaborate, but decaying, woodwork that resembles its once glorious decor.

I've never been to a church service, but I've heard some stories from the Bible. The ark and the rainbow coat. My sister doesn't believe in a God, neither does my dad. I'm not sure what my mom believes since she left before I could ask her. Maybe she's why I don't believe.

My feet echo and give birth to the idea that there are things walking up the walls, in step with me. The shadows contort into hunched over beings with lengthy limbs. They're watching me. The curious human-spider shadows lurk in the corners of my vision as I pass. My hands grip the edges of my shorts to help quash my fear, but it doesn't work.

There are only half the pews left and one has been up-turned, broken in the middle, like someone was angry that they could only steal half a set of benches from a church. Two short steps up from the floor where I stand is an altar with a haunting shadow behind it. Made up of stacked sharp edges—that jut into the ceiling— the altar looks like a castle etched from ivory, transforming into crosses. The windows depict tragic scenes in colored glass and, curiously, they don't paint the room in red, green, and gold, like I'd expect. The light is pure white and shimmers on the dusty floor as I shuffle through, making as little sound as I can.

The door beside the castle structure doesn't budge. I follow the wall of the sanctuary until I'm on the other side, near a curved balcony, shaking and eventually kicking the two other doors I find. There are staircases on both sides that lead up to the balcony, and I'm not about to venture up. I go back to the door I came from, and I pull. I pull harder. The damn door doesn't budge and I'm sweating from the effort. The summer definitely didn't forget to heat this room.

I frantically attack all the other doors, completely forgetting that I was trying to be quiet. The room is swirling with dust from the air I'm generating by running back and forth, and I cough and gag as it congeals in my lungs. I'm forced to climb the stairs.

Maybe it's just my fear getting the better of me because I have to fight my legs to move to the next step. My heart pumps so wildly I'm dizzy from too much oxygen, and when I grip the railing it snaps at my weight. I stumble and hit the edge of the step with my forearm—which I'm guessing is already pooling with blood under the skin, and turning purple in a large round. I exhale sharply and it's winter; my breath is in front of my face like a low cloud. The dust is everywhere. At my feet a roach twitches, upside-down amongst chunks of ceiling that litter my path. I leave foot—also a hand and elbow—prints on the stairs as I go up, and all I can think about is getting home to have a hot shower.

A light reflects off the wall in front of me, reminding me of a firefly when you want to catch it, flipping back and forth with a brighter ring in the center. I'm convinced it isn't natural. It's a flashlight, and I'm dead. The thugs after my sister somehow got inside and they're going to find me. The ring in the light gets brighter. I beg my legs to move. Move!

I run back down the stairs with as much care to noise as I can, but the thumping of my worn Nikes is hard to conceal as a wave of panic crashes into me. My hair sticks to my neck, and every time I wipe it out of my face my hand becomes slick with sweat, making it impossible to get a hold of the door knob. There are footsteps on the stairs, light and slow. I look from the stairs to the row of benches, back again to the stairs, until I forget which direction is up. I turn and dive behind a pew, peeking out with only as much of my face as absolutely necessary. There is only a tiny sliver of the stairs in my line of sight.

The figure's shadow appears on the wall as they descend the stairs. My hands aches with cold fear. Thick air burns my eyes and I blink, straining to see. I missed something. The shadow is gone, but I never saw it go back up the stairs. Swallowing is impossible, so I spit what's in my mouth across the aisle. That will, most definitely, send me to the burning fires of hell.

I wait. For as long as I can stand it, I wait. Until I notice the shadows have danced to new places on the floor, I finally get up. Once again, I creep to each door and quietly try to dislodge them, when the one across from where I entered gives way, I slide myself into the new hallway in relief.

The walls are lined with windows washed in dirt, an almost mirror of the other side of the church. The late afternoon sun beats into my cheek as I rub at the caked on sweaty dust that's turning hard and dry. It doesn't come off easily and I resort to scratching at it, cringing at the dirty build up forming under my fingernails. A chair sits sideways halfway down the hall, covered in layers of filth from a leak in the ceiling. I look up just as a few bits of debris make their way down, they land on my nose and in my eye. Rubbing never makes it better, but I can't help the itchy feeling, or shake the thought that I'm going to go blind. I bury my knuckles into my eyeball until it hurts. Scratching sounds flutter across the floor and I whip around in surprise, expecting a person, but only see a tiny tail disappear into a room behind me.

"What are you doing in here?"

CHAPTER THREE

I'M STILL LOOKING behind me when I hear the voice. The scream that comes from me is loud, and resonates through my entire body. I back up as a boy, standing twenty feet away, trips backwards and lands inside an empty, metal tub. The tub is half inside the last room in the hallway, like someone had given up trying to take it. His laugh rips through the room and fills it with life, but I'm shaking uncontrollably.

"What the hell is wrong with you?" I scream, then realize how much attention from outside all the noise inside may have caused. I assume my eyes are bugging out of my skull because the boy's face is making a similar expression.

"What is it?" He's whispering, sensing the fear that's radiating from me.

It's all too much. The boy, the thugs outside, the creepy church. I suck in a chest full of air and let out a giant sob. With my arms crushing my into myself, I whisper, "There are guys outside who are going to kill me!"

The boy scrambles out of the tub and runs toward me, nearly taking just my arm with him when he pulls me back up the hallway, into the sanctuary. We climb the stairs by twos, and he lets go of my hand when we reach the top. My shoulder hurts and I rub it as I stand where he left me. I just want to go home.

He slides ungracefully across the floor, slipping by a huge window and falling onto his side, barely missing a box with his head. He chuckles and sits up on his knees, peering out into the courtyard. Next to the window his presence is laughable; the decorative framed glass takes up nearly the entire wall, all the way to the ceiling point.

"I'm pretty sure they aren't getting in here anytime soon. The one can't walk without tripping."

My arm is getting sore from the pinching I can't seem to stop. Wake up.

"Why are you in here?" I ask through chattering teeth.

He looks back over his shoulder and stares for a beat too long. His eyes, so green they glow, are soft and concerned. He reaches behind the box for something. I watch his eyes, still focused on mine, and I can't blink. He walks back toward me, sending me into shock with the sudden fear of imminent death. I'm immobile—floating inside my own head—ready for the knife he probably has to slide easily across my throat.

"You get used to the creepy." He throws a hoodie over my head and it's warm, smelling like an earthy cologne that awkwardly grounds me in reality. My head pops through and he's so close, smiling like this happens all the time, with his soft square face. If I had to guess his age, I'd say not much older than I am.

He runs a hand through his dark hair and it jets out in all directions, "I'm Niven."

"Brenna." There's a pause before I ask him, again, why he's here.

"I don't like it at home." His expression is light, but I hear something sad in his voice that he's trying to hide.

I walk to the window just as Danny hauls back and rams his hand across his friend's cheek. Nate stumbles and holds his face; blood dripping between his fingers and down the back of his hand. I can hear random words that make it up to us, *locked door* and *impossible.*

"Get down," Niven whispers, and pulls me to kneel beside him. It's hard to see through the warped glass at the edges of the frames, and as I try to find the right spot I knock temples with him. He holds his head with an embarrassed smirk. He's staring, so I find the pockets in the hoodie and occupy myself with making a comfortable place for my hands.

"Thanks." It comes out with a hiccup. My cheeks warm as I continue to stare at my knees. He doesn't say anything, just keeps an eye out the window. I look back out and hear a truck start in the distance. I watch the dust clutter the air as they drive away.

"They didn't find the loose window."

"I came in that window," I say. "It locked behind me or something. The basement is gross."

"You were in the basement?" His eyes are so bright I wonder where the light that reflects in them is coming from. His heads tilts slightly, studying me.

"I fell in."

"That's not the window I was talking about anyway. There's one past the bathtub that's unlocked."

"Good to know." I get up and brush off my shins.

"Oh." He slumps slightly, sitting on his feet with an arm draped across the dusty window sill. His eyes are focused on his fingers that are tapping a tune on the marble as his face ever so slightly contorts in thought.

I have to get home to make sure Mabel is okay, but my stomach sinks when I think about him being all alone. It's not like my house is anything I want to be running back to, "What time is it?"

He smiles. "Only a quarter past four."

"Why here?" I sit back down, crisscrossing my legs.

"It's quiet."

"And creepy." I shiver.

"And creepy." He smiles wide. Almost inhumanly wide.

"I take it you like creepy then?"

He crawls beside me and reaches back toward the box. He pulls out a sketchbook from a backpack, sitting back down slightly closer than he was before, and flips open the spiral bound book. It's half on his, half on my lap.

"I like creepy." He's pointing to a drawing of arms reaching from the walls in the hallway where we met, they grab at the air searching for their next victim to walk by. The smell of fresh paper drifts up as he flips through the pages. I hate limbs, and unattached body parts, and other visually disturbing things, but his drawings aren't so bad. I smash my eyes together in a few hard blinks, to keep my brain from creating some elaborate horror story to go along with the drawings.

"I guess I do too." I hesitate because I don't let anyone read my stories. The purple journal I keep them in is at home so I don't see the harm in it. "I write stories. No one reads them, but I write them anyway. One is about a murderer, sort of."

"I'd read them." His face is full of honesty, and I'm not used to that reaction. I'm not used to any reaction; most people think I'm weird so they bump me in the halls at school or trip me when I get on the bus. I love that it's summer break.

"Yeah right. They suck anyway."

He smiles to himself and I wonder what he's thinking. He looks up through his lashes at me, still smiling, then puts the book away. He crawls back toward the window and looks out.

"Do you ever feel like you're more alone when you're out there surrounded by other people?"

I feel like that a lot. Especially when my sister is around. She attracts all the wrong kinds of people, and in turn makes my life miserable. I'm always caught in the middle of saving her or running. Not that she ever needs me, really. I lift my eyes from my dirty nails to Niven and realize he's been watching me consider his question. I nod. He smiles. He does that a lot.

After a long silence I apologize for being a conversational dud, and with a shake of his head he quiets me, "It's nice. I don't feel like I have to talk either."

We sit in silence again, and he picks out something from his backpack. In the growing darkness I see a stick with a jagged ball hanging from the end and imagine a medieval flail. He's been buttering me up just to practice whacking me with a strange old weapon because, honestly, that's what boys who hang out in abandoned churches alone do. It catches the light, and I see it's a large water bottle with a grocery bag caught to the end that just sags sadly with its sharp lumpy contents. He separates the two and folds the bag down to act like a bowl.

"Candy?"

"Isn't that the first rule of 'Stranger Danger' stuff you're taught in pre-school?" I blurt out. "Don't take candy from strangers." I'm not really serious, but he shrugs and pulls the bag back to his lap.

"Oh well, more for me then." I see a smile twitching on his lips as he peruses the variety of sweet delights before him. I sit uncomfortably for a minute before I see a tiny red bag and can't help myself, I crawl on the disgusting floor and sit myself directly beside him.

I put out my hand. "Skittles please."

He dangles it above me, so I grab it from him with a quick swipe. I rip the bag at the corner and pour half of the little chewy pebbles into my mouth savoring the initial flavor rush.

"Are these old?" I look at the bag all over for a date. The grapes taste like lemon or something completely not grape; I didn't even see anything yellow fall out of the bag.

"Last Halloween, so probably." He shrugs and puts an entire full size Kit-Kat in his mouth. I stare because he doesn't have a Steven Tyler sized mouth, but he just ate the whole candy bar and I'm impressed.

I'd seen a lot of that large pair of lips, because I'd watched a lifetime of music videos. My dad wasn't into sports, games, or grilling —just music. He'd always wished his band would make it big. They were an old-school rock sound with a lazy drunken look that, of course, never made it anywhere on time and then never made a cent. I remember being six years old outside of a club with my sister. We watched as our intoxicated father stumbled out the back door and knocked over a trash can, spilling beer bottles and Styrofoam boxes everywhere. They avalanched onto the ground by our feet, getting stringy nacho cheese all over my new gym shoes. I'd never been more upset about anything in my life before. Or since. It's a pretty small thing to be so angry about, but when you're six you're overly passionate. So, I started expecting much less of people shortly after that, and just don't let any of it upset me. Everyone lets you down eventually.

Niven hands me his drawing pad and a pen, "I think you need to get some of that out of your head."

I eye him, dubious of the way he seems to sense my mood, and shake my head. I'm always the perceptive one, and I've never been around anyone else who gave a shit; I usually assume I'm the only person I'll ever meet who pays attention to facial expressions.

"Man, have you ever looked in a mirror?" he asks. "Your eyes flit around like there's multiple people trying to use them at once."

He pauses, his face twisting into a grimace. "You're totally crazy aren't you?"

"No."

"You're totally a writer then."

"What do you mean by that?"

"You're going off on tangents in your head right now, aren't you?"

"No." But I do.

"You think super crazy things, and then realize you were imagining it."

"Sometimes." My mouth twists up in defense. "Doesn't everyone?"

"I doubt it."

"You don't?"

"I guess I do." He looks down at his sketch book and fights an embarrassed smile.

His head dips while he contemplates the spiral ring of the

book, and I notice how lanky his frame seems. His jeans fit him perfectly—even when he's sitting I notice—and look more comfortable than my shorts, but his gray tee shirt hangs like it has nothing to grip to. I tilt my head to see what his face is doing, but he puts his hand up and leans on it, away from me.

"My dad says I'm crazy like my Uncle Dan."

"How's he crazy?" I ask.

"He hears voices and all that shit. I don't hear voices." He looks at me, straight into me. "I swear I'm not crazy, don't freak out."

"That's probably the worst thing you can say when you don't want someone to freak out!" I yell, unnerved, as my eyebrows jump toward my hairline.

Then I smile, and he does too. We break into fits of laughter and it feels good after all the disturbing happenings of the day. Really, it feels good for the first time all summer. I look out the window, paranoid they are coming back, only this time with sledge hammers and lighters. The vision of being trapped in a balcony while the church goes up in flames makes me shiver even in Niven's hoodie.

"I only have my dad and sister, the rest of my relatives split town as soon as they could. I don't even know any of them," I say. "I barely remember my mother."

"Does it matter?"

"Does what matter?" I ask.

"Are you worse off because she's gone?"

I've asked myself that question so many times. "I can't really say, I don't have anything to compare it to."

He squints and nods, like he approves of my vague answer.

"I should get going." After such an interesting piece of afternoon with him I hate to just leave, but if I don't make it home it may turn into a disastrous evening. There isn't anything good on T.V. on Saturdays.

"Sure."

I get up and brush off my pants before turning toward the stairs.

"Hey." He hesitates and I know he wants to ask me something, and I know what it is. It's the same thing I want to ask him.

"Yeah?"

He scratches the back of his head. "I come here all the time. Like, all the time."

I nod. "Maybe tomorrow."

He smiles.

CHAPTER FOUR

I FIND MY way down the stairs, and out the loose window in the rotted out bathroom. The summer air turned cold while I was inside, and I'm glad for Niven's hoodie—something warm to walk home in. My walk will be the second best part of the night, because as soon as I get home, it's back to real life.

I peer around corners cautiously, and duck into alleys in case someone sees me. It's what I have to do; I look a lot like my sister and she gets into a lot of trouble. There's always someone looking for her. Plus, Danny and Nate are still around.

Our city is big, not population wise—just acreage really—but somehow it makes me claustrophobic. Building after building it's all the same; dirty windows and old paint decorate the streets. Old cars, busted street lights, and a strong smell of sewer accompany me home. I pass a few chain fast food places, and an adult video store, before I make it to our tiny one-way street. The setting sun burns hot spots in the road through chain link fences and coats the side of my body in warmth. I don't see my dad's truck, but I have a feeling he's home. He's almost always home by now.

The gate to our yard is hanging open, oddly contorted, and hasn't functioned properly in over a year. I'm not too worried about it though. When are criminals ever stopped by a three and a half foot tall rusted fence? A surge of anger at my father's negligence hits me, and I kick the thing closed as I pass. Dry dirt mists the air around my feet as I cross the unpaved driveway. Dad's green pickup is parked ridiculously in the backyard. The likelihood of him being in the living room, passed out drunk, eases the tension I didn't know I had built up in my jaw. I take the four steps to the back stoop in one leap, and quietly let myself inside.

"Girl, is that you?" His rough voice hits like a fist to my side, and I instinctively move around the room like I've been home for hours. He lumps into the kitchen, scratching his stubbly beard that barely hides the scar on his chin, stopping before he gets to me. His eyes are bloodshot from an entire afternoon of drinking and watching TV, most likely, but it could be something more. "Where's Mabel?"

"She left me out at the gas station, by the clinic," I say, trying to keep the humiliation in my voice to a minimum.

"What?" he yells. "Why is she there? She get knocked up already? She's only sixteen!"

"She's eighteen, Dad. I'm sixteen."

"Damn it."

"And no." I add, and I know what's going to happen before I say it. "She's just looking for love in all the wrong places. She clearly has daddy issues."

But I say it anyway, attempting to put my face completely inside my shoulder, but his hand connects with my cheek, and I taste blood. The skin by my right eye burns and my jaw is already numb and stiff. I open and close it, hoping it won't swell shut.

"Don't you talk about your sister like that."

It's not like he cares, or that he thinks it isn't true. He just has a lot of drunken rage. He also has a soft spot for slapping me, because he assumes when I open my mouth it's going to piss him off. To be fair, most of it does. But when I have nothing to show for my sixteen years of life, aside from a proficiency in sarcasm and quips, I can't come up with a single reason to reign in my thoughts. A fat lip isn't much, considering it could be worse. And has been worse.

Tears roll down my cheeks from the pain, and I'm ready to let some seriously hateful things fly out of my mouth, but the phone interrupts my thoughts. He backs up to answer, keeping an eye on me as he leans into the wall with the receiver. Grunts and nods are all I hear of the conversation.

"Yeah, she's not here." He grips the phone tighter. "I don't care how important it is, I don't know where she is. Get lost."

That last bit seems directed at me, but even if it isn't, I

dart down the hall to my bedroom anyway, slamming the door behind me. The thick blanket I nailed in front of the window blocks out nearly every ounce of light, blinding me as I feel around in the dark. During the summer I sleep well past the sun, and its horrible glaring heat, at least until I have to crawl out of bed for food. I peek around the edge of the rough flannel and find the moon already halfway into the sky, even before the sun has set completely, with a hazy black edge like a burned piece of paper. I drop the blanket, collapsing onto my floor bound mattress, frustrated and drained. Frank Allen's face pops into my mind and open my eyes to erase it from my vision; I don't want to think about how Mabel destroys everything for me.

She's not a notorious thief or con-artist, well, maybe she kind of is. But she's not scamming companies, only their stupidest customers. She likes to hang around places that have young male clientele who like to party. Sometimes she makes me come along, a promise of cash dangled in my face, but it's never enough for the crap I have to get out of. Sometimes the promises are just plain empty, and I end up dragging myself out of a gutter, literally.

One time she shoved her portion of magic mushrooms down my throat so the pack of fat-wallet-high-seekers would think she was tripping too. I had already, mistakenly, ingested what I was given so I all but blacked out, leaving the group and walking nine miles away. I woke up the next morning covered in mud and leaves, unable to remember anything that happened. I was just glad to be alive. Later, she told me I was screaming about the repo man coming to take my organs, and that I walked off trying to sing Sarah Brightman songs. I asked why she didn't come after me and it was obscure excuse after ridiculous excuse. The main reason being, she hadn't gotten to their money by that point and I wasn't important enough to worry about.

I rolled onto the laminate wood floor and let the surface cool my burning cheek. After that whole side of the road experience, I make sure to never get in the car with her and strangers. I try not to go anywhere with her or be somewhere she might end up, but there are only so many places within walking distance of my house.

My door suddenly looks like it's going to fly into the room, shaking with audible force.

"You come get me if she gets home." My dad pounds on the other side with a fist, his voice coming through muffled, and I stick my tongue out from the safety of the shadows. I fall asleep spread eagle on the floor feeling a bit like dead fish, only without the scales, just to be woke up an hour later by the sounds of Mabel climbing in the window. The house is a two bedroom, so the fact that she sleeps on the other side of the room is unavoidable.

She whispers, "You're like a cat or something."

"Says the girl climbing in windows."

"You always find your way home." I huff so strongly at the statement that spit flies out of my mouth and lands on the floor in a tiny light reflecting puddle. I push myself back onto my mattress and grab the first thing I can to throw in her direction, which is only a pair of jeans, and I'm not even sure I hit her since I can't see her.

"What? It's true."

"You're so insane," I say, not bothering to whisper.

"Hush," she says, "I was supposed to take him to the bar with me tonight and he's going to be pissed I left him."

"Insane," I reiterate.

"Just because you don't understand what—" She begins a speech. I don't want to hear it. I sit up and smack my hand to the wall.

"You wouldn't..." She breathes in the darkness.

I bang on the wall with both my fists. "DAD!"

"Stop!"

"DAD! MABEL IS HOME!"

"You little bitch!" I hear her shoes tap twice on the floor and then she's on top of me pulling at my hair like the prissy girl she is.

"That's what you're going to be when Dad gets through with you."

We struggle for a while, trying not to be hurt while also trying to severely hurt the other when finally I get a foot under her and shove. She hits the floor hard and we're panting like we've just out run the cops.

"Maybe... he's... dead." She says through breaths and I have a moment of joy before my heart sinks and I wonder if it will always be that way—to wish him gone but not want him to really be dead.

"Probably just drunk."

She grunts in agreement.

"And I'm pretty sure you meant pigeon," I say, with unintended snobbery.

"What?" I hear her crawl to her bed.

"Homing pigeon. Not cat."

CHAPTER FIVE

I WAKE UP half-way off my bed with a note on my face. Mabel left to see a friend early and I have to keep an eye on Dad. Fat Chance.

I wad up the note and chew on it before spitting it into her bed, flipping up the blankets to cover it. When I reach for the doorknob I reconsider the spit-drenched present and walk back to her bed. Then I think about the ditch I woke up in, spin on my toes and march out the door.

Dad is asleep in the armchair in the living room when I peek around the corner, and I'm sure that's more than enough keeping an eye on him. The room is dark except for the light that spills in from the kitchen windows behind me, a little red glow from his chair catches my attention. The cigarette could easily fall to the floor, catch our dirty green carpet on fire, and slowly burn the whole house down. The decision to walk over and pluck it from his comatose fingers doesn't take nearly as long as I would have liked. He fell asleep just after lighting it; it's half ash. The gray flakes flutter to the floor after a twitch of my thumb and I pull in a long, thick lungful. The smoke billows out of my mouth, I watch it drift to the ceiling before I put it out on back of his chair and drop it in his lap. Nasty.

The kitchen is the brightest place in the house, it looks out into the back yard and gives a great view of all the neighbors' back doors. I take a glass out of the cabinet beside the window and gaze outside as I fill it with water. So many of the stories I write have to do with these people, most of whom I don't even know.

Watching out the window, I imagine a swat team pull up on the road running parallel to ours, they surround the house directly behind us, some hiding in the overgrown field that is the owner's back yard. The sagging section of the roof suddenly explodes, and pieces hit the siding of our house. Bright fire engulfs the little yellow home as men break windows and call out to each other with commands I can't hear.

Dad coughs and I snap out of my head. I hear him grumble, then fall back asleep. There isn't much actual food in my fridge: condiments, beer, blocks of moldy cheese, and some milk. The milk isn't expired, so I pour a bowl of stale fruit loops and soak them in it. I stand at the window until I'm done, trying to not envision the neighbor's house ablaze.

As I'm rinsing the thick salmon colored bowl I see Mrs. Peters standing in her yard, watching her tiny dog find a place to relive itself. She looks toward the kitchen window like someone called to her, her eyes squinting in the mid-day sun, but she gives up with a shake of her head when no one appears. I check the other side of the house wondering if I can see anyone, but the yards are empty.

I hate being on edge all the time. It used to be okay, until Mabel screwed over a few too many guys and now they know where she lives. It's not like Dad is going to come to the rescue if someone comes looking for her. Even if he was sober, he'd probably just trade us for more beer.

An engine cuts off outside, and I'm sure it's just my paranoia but can't help it. I duck into the dark corner of the living room to hide. The wooden steps out front creak and moan as feet march to the top, and I slide down the wall to hug my knees. They beat the door with angry fists.

"Mabel! We know you're in there!"

It's Danny, I can tell by the little bit of Mississippi in his voice. I wonder how long he's been in Kentucky to not have gained a different. Dad stirs in the recliner in front of me. I help him along by kicking the bar on the side of the chair, sending his feet crashing to the ground and jolting him awake.

"What in the hell?" He drops a bottle and it rolls toward me on the floor behind his chair.

The men have apparently had enough because I can see the knob jiggle with every shoulder smashed into the door. He lumbers over to answer, but not before picking up the baseball bat he keeps near the window. His silhouette is tall, and mostly thin, with a slight baby beer bump as he leans onto the metal stick with confidence. The deadbolt clicks as he cracks the door, letting light stream into the room like a knife cutting through soft fruit.

"What do ya want?" He's slurring and my hiding spot suddenly seems less safe.

"Where's Mabel old man?" The second guy is leaning over his friend, into the house for a better look.

"Get outta here." He's shutting them out, but Danny sticks his foot in the opening and gives a good shove, catching my Dad off balance and stumbling backwards into the room. I gasp as the sound of metal hitting flesh rings through the room; it's sickening. Dad swings the bat and hits Nate square in the head, sending him sprawling across the floor in a rag doll heap. Danny catches my eye in the dark; the light from the door shimmers off my glittering high-tops, giving me away. I scramble for things to propel me forward, like walls and chairs, but he's on me in a second with a handful of my hair in his hand.

"I told you I'd get you." It feels like my scalp is separating from my skull, I'm screaming but I can't form words. I call out for my Daddy in desperation, feeling a chunk of my curls detaching; I want him to save me.

A loud, stomach-turning crack echoes in the kitchen, and my attacker is wailing on the ground holding his knee.

"What are you two involved in?"

"Nothing Daddy." Tears are in my eyes, streaming out from all the pain.

He grabs me by the arm, "What is going on here?"

I wrestle with his grasp, unsuccessfully, pleading to be set free.

Nate groans from the living room and adrenaline courses through me. My arm feels light. I'm unrestrained. I take the opportunity to get out the back door, and I trip down the stairs rolling and falling face first into the grass.

"Honey," Mrs. Peters calls from her side of the fence. "Is everything okay?"

"Call 911! Tell them two men broke into my house!" I yell as I take off down the driveway.

It's like being in a bubble, I can't hear anything but my heart and I don't see anything for what it is. Everything is distorted and shiny. I run, I don't even know what direction I'm headed in until I see the familiar purple logo on the sign post. My body is on fire when I stop cold in front of the glass door, and walk into the public library out of breath and looking like a fish that escaped a net. I could have just gotten out of a pool for all anyone knew. Taking a deep breath, I steady myself with the shelf in the first aisle I come to, and try not to drip sweat on anything.

"Brenna?" I turn, startled, to find a kid from my gym class standing behind me. His loose textured brown curls cover his eyebrows which rise sky high when he looks me over. His khaki shorts look like the pockets are full of something, but I couldn't even guess as to what since he seems to be on the clock putting away books.

"Wyatt?" I slip when I try to reposition myself and he laughs.

"Are you okay?" He's reading spines from a cart at his side.

"I'm fine," I breathe. "I didn't know you work here."

"Yeah, great summer job. I like seeing all these books I wouldn't have otherwise known about. I've read some interesting stuff in the past month." He reaches as far as he can to a shelf above his head, stretching his arm and standing on the tips of his toes. The book teeters, nearly falling back onto his face, but he bounces once to fit it in place perfectly.

I slide down the metal edge of the end of the book shelf and rest my head on my knees. Every muscle in my back hurts, and my stomach is turning around in all the wrong directions. I'm actually afraid to ever go home. I don't have any way to contact Mabel to warn her, but then I wonder if I'd want to if I could. She's my sister but sometimes it might be better to let nature take its course. I shake my head, hating myself.

"We close in a half hour, want to hang out?" He's still putting books away, like it's no big deal he just asked to hang out. We talked at school all the time, but we never seemed to take that extra step toward being actual friends. I'm not even sure I'm capable of having friends. Every time I try Mabel ruins it.

"Sure, if you don't mind that two giant douche bags are

trying to kill me." I'm sure he's curious about my waterlogged style, and I can't hold it all in forever. "I'm not even sure what Mabel stole from them, but it's really fucking important."

"She's something." Is all he says.

"Mom, I've got a friend over." Wyatt drops his backpack just inside the door from the garage and peeks around the corners of his house. "Nobody home." He shrugs.

"Cool." I look at my sparkling purple shoes—the only gift from Mabel I've ever accepted—glistening in the sunlight streaming from the decorative glass front door. He leads us through the kitchen, down a hallway into his room, and it looks eerily like my own. The windows are covered with a couple black sheets, even though the rest of the house sports expensive curtains and elaborate rods, and his mattress takes up one corner of the room. The opposite wall is lined with Swedish self-assembled bookshelves that have space for barely a handful more books. When he flips the light switch I realize the books are color coordinated and have a moment of breathlessness.

"You have not read all of those." I demand.

"No, but I have read over two thirds of them." He starts emptying his pockets into a jar on the dresser at the foot of his bed. It's full of change, marbles, keys, fossils, teeth... and bones. The body parts look to be from small animals, not humans, thankfully.

"I used to read a lot." I say, scanning the titles.

"What changed?" He flops down onto his bed, exhausted.

"Life." I'm really not sure what changed actually.

"I think too much, so I read for a distraction."

"From what?"

"Can you believe school starts in three weeks?" He asks from inside his pillow, and I turn to stare blankly at him and his obvious redirection. It's difficult to not ask him again. He reads to not think about it, so I'm sure he doesn't want to talk about it.

"I guess." I grab a book about Angels and Demons. The spine is worn and the cover is uninteresting. I put it back.

"How far back can you remember?" He asks. "Like to when you were four or five maybe?"

Pausing at a black tome with no title, I concentrate on his question. The most distant memory I have is the garbage on my shoes outside the club when I was six. I tell him the story and he contemplates it while lying on his back, hands cradling his head.

"I just don't remember much of anything. Nothing before third grade really." He's talking to the ceiling and doesn't see me pick up a fossil that's sitting alone on the shelf in front of the few purple novels. The grey rock has a multi legged bug's outline indented in it, and it doesn't look like anything I've ever seen before. Legs and antennae sticking out in all directions—it kind of makes me sick.

"At least you don't have parental hatred as a result of those memories... since you don't have them that is." I place the creepy stone back on the shelf.

Wyatt closes his eyes, "Sometimes I feel like I could remember things but I've blocked it or something."

I shrug not knowing what to say to him. There aren't magical things to make you regain memories. None that I know of anyway. If we were in a cartoon I could take his baseball bat that's sitting in the corner, and with a good wind up crack it right across his skull. He'd probably only wobble at the blow, and with a shake of his head all those things once lost would come flooding back. I smile when I realize how right Niven was about my strange imagination.

"How long have you worked at the library?" I ask.

"This is my second summer, it's pretty easy." He's still on his back relaxing.

"I wouldn't care if I was shoveling horse shit into buckets," I say. "I just need to get a paycheck."

I suddenly feel kind of awkward being in his room and knowing nothing at all about him. I glance at the next shelf, and see a picture of little Wyatt with, I assume, his much older brother.

"Where's he?" I hold up the picture and I don't even have to hear an answer. The look Wyatt has on his face says it all. He's dead.

"I don't even remember him that well. Everyone, even my parents, thinks he ran away, but..."

He turns over in his bed, and I'm not sure if he's crying or something else equally awkward. I wouldn't know how to console him about his dead brother when I've wished my sister dead multiple times a day. I'd be such a hypocrite. So instead, I just stand, digging my shoe into a hole in the red toned wood floors.

He rolls back over to face me and smiles, "Want to go somewhere cool?"

After a few miles, I give up asking where we're headed, I know I'll probably figure it out soon anyway. He talks about his mom's weird obsession with internet games, and how she's constantly farming, or solving mysteries, when she's not sleeping or at work. It seems similar to my situation, aside from the violent outbursts. Both our parents have unhealthy habits that consume them.

We end up at the church, and by then I'm beyond curious. Does he know Niven?

"Why are we here?" I ask, innocently.

"I've had dreams about this place and I swear something happened here, something to do with my brother. One time I was here, and I looked in the window, and I'm sure I saw a tail escaping through the doorway."

"A tail? Like a rat? Because there were rats in there for sure." The pink tail flashes in my mind just before Niven's eyes. My stomach flips in on itself, and I feel a rush of adrenaline at the memory of their vibrant color. I can't help the smile on my face and I'm not sure why, I barely know the guy.

"You've been in there?" Wyatt is stunned, and I don't

blame him, the place is creepy as hell from the outside. Not that it's any less creepy inside either.

"Sort of," The urge to keep Niven a secret courses through my veins and I immediately redirect the conversation. "It's all broken and dirty in there. I was hiding from those guys I told you about."

I look around purposefully and grab Wyatt's hand, "Can we head out? Please? I'm not looking forward to seeing them again." I show him a growing bruise on my side from where I hit something when I fell into the basement.

"Shit, I'm sorry. I didn't know." He shoves his free hand through his shaggy hair and backs away from the church, his fingers still linked in my own. I find an opportunity to untangle our digits hoping he doesn't notice. I straighten my shirt just in case he does.

"It's a creepy place, maybe you just have vivid dreams." I offer.

"No." He's determined to remember whatever it is he lost and I can't blame him. Even though I can't stand her, if I thought I knew something about my sister's death I wouldn't want to feel like it was a stolen memory.

CHAPTER SIX

I CRASH INTO my bed like it's midnight when it's only mid-afternoon. My pillows hug my face, the bed is too comfortable to leave, so I stay as long as I can. But all too soon there comes the banging on the door.

"Brenna..." He drags out my name, and I know he wants me to make him food. I roll out of bed, pulling my hair back into a crazy ponytail. The room is dark, and the light that pours in when I open the door is disorienting.

"Is your sister home?" Dad asks as I blink forcefully, adjusting to the florescent kitchen light mixed with bright setting sun. Purple and red blotches pepper the side of his face, and I gasp reflexively. His eye is puffy but other than that he appears okay.

"What happened? Didn't you have a bat? Did Mrs. Peters call the police?" My questions come out as one breathe I can't hold in.

"Oh." He touches at the swollen skin on his head. "I fell out of my truck. Those little shits that grabbed you are in the hospital, or at least one is."

I sigh, relief filling me—I'm glad I didn't have anything to do with his injuries. Not that I had anything to do with the break-in either.

He closes his eyes, and leans against the door frame near my head. His wrinkles are clearly visible when they are so close, but he seems so young when you can't see them. I'm surprised all the drinking hasn't destroyed his skin, or given him premature hair loss. His brown hair is still full and greasy, resembling styles like 90's band members, semi-long and free flowing. His t-shirt is torn from the scuffle earlier, and his sweatpants are well worn, but at least he doesn't smell as bad as he usually does.

"Baby, I hurt." He doesn't bother opening his eyes and I'm grateful—my facial expressions would put him into a rage. I roll my eyes at his pathetic request, and pat his shoulder before ducking back into the room to search for pain meds; Mabel's second favorite thing to steal. First, of course, is cash. Untraceable cash. I find a stash of Percocet and dump three into my hand to take to him. He's standing in the kitchen when I come back.

"You're my favorite, do I ever tell you that?" He says as I drop three little pills into his palm. He dry swallows two, then smashes the third into powder with his pocket knife. The fine granules spread across the counter top, like sand leveling in an hourglass. I imagine myself trapped inside, drowning in tiny particles, like Jasmine from the Disney movie. His long, loud inhale snaps me out of my thoughts.

"Jesus, Dad." Instinctively, I lunge under him, and guide him to his recliner. His eyes droop, and I realize he hadn't been sober when he took the pills. The combination will knock him out for hours, if it doesn't kill him first. His skin is tacky from sweat, and I wonder if it will ever *not* be like this. I don't want to spend every day waiting for the back of his hand across my cheek, or the color in his face to eventually turn pale and gray. When I finally leave, he'll be on his own for stolen narcotics.

The room seems hazy even with the sun coming through the blinds full force. Dust spins and floats around in the air, making my lungs heavy with the thought of breathing it in. Dad's mouth hangs open, drool spilling down the side of his chin, and I just want to get out.

A long walk later, I'm standing in front of the loose window, debating turning around to go home. A noise from the trees, behind the church, startles me out of my internal argument and into another one: whether or not I should go see what it is.

"It was a deer." I hear his voice before I see him. He's walking from around the front with his backpack, a book, and a smile larger than seems possible for his mouth.

"Hi." I squeak.

"Hey." His voice soothes my knotted stomach and shaking hands. I didn't even notice I was nervous.

After a minute of staring at each other, he explains, "It's great light for drawing, so I was out by the tree line." I nod in agreement.

We climb in the window, and stand around the room awkwardly, where pipes stick up out of the floor, rusted shut into stationary weapons. There's a toilet broken in half, jagged and covered in ceiling particles, perched in the corner like a crumbling statue.

"I saw you here earlier." The broken silence isn't made better by this, at all.

"Yeah?" I ask, wondering if he's jealous, but then questioning why I should care.

"Did you tell him I come here?"

"No."

He smiles and takes my hand. We go back up to the balcony, where it seems that some of his stuff stays permanently. His back muscles flex under his tight shirt as he slides off the backpack and starts to dig something out.

Shuffling noises from below float up to where we stand, creeping into my ears like tiny ants, and send my heart beating through my chest. I turn so quickly I lose my balance, but Niven catches me easily. "Just rats."

His nearness keeps my already elevated heart rate going strong. No matter what I tell myself it continues to punch at my ribcage, and I don't know if it was the noise or him. He smiles. It's a warm, comforting kind of smile and with it all my tension melts away.

He sits with his back to the window. It's glowing from the mid-day sun, and fills the air with a nice heat. It counter-acts the ill feeling the abandoned building gives off. I ease into a more comfortable state, and know a little better why he chooses to spend time in such a place.

"Can I see what you were drawing?" I reach down for his book, but he pulls it back. There's a smirk threatening to twist his mouth around, and it's hard not to stare as his lips twitch in amusement. I grab at it again, but he jumps up, holding it above my head.

"I want to read your stories first." He grins wide, and his head towers over me. I hadn't realized he was so tall.

"What?" I step back, playing at anger. "I don't even know where my notebook is."

"Yes you do. You're such a liar." He glares at me.

I am lying, but is it that obvious?

"Fine. Next time. Can I see your stuff now?" He's hesi-tant, and still trying to be flirtatious. He smiles and bounds off behind me toward an elaborate carved corner. Ten feet up the dark wooden column is a little ledge that I'm guessing used to hold a statue or something similar, but now it's empty. He climbs using the tiny indents to place his fingers and shoes, and sits the book flat on the shelf.

"Now I can't be tempted to let you look. I want to read your stuff first." He hops down and sends dust flying when his feet hit the floor—it circles around him like he controls it.

"That's lame." I shove my hands in my pockets, and kick a piece of ceiling across the floor.

"We could explore."

"The church?" I ask, surprised.

"Yeah, why not? I've barely been anywhere in here."

Considering there are two of us, and nothing likely living in the place other than a few rats, I'm surprised at my own lack of curiosity. To be honest, I'm more curious about where he inherited his extraterrestrial green eyes.

"Come on." He takes my hand again, and I'm flooded with emotions I've never felt. Of course I've had crushes before, but something feels different about this, less intrinsic. My senses are heightened, and it's making me dizzy to think about anything too complex. I just follow him blindly down the stairs.

"Last time I tried, all the doors were stuck." I mention this as we cross the lower level, to the hall with blacked out windows. The hallway that leads to the grungy basement.

"Well, there are two of us now, and one is a big strong man." He flexes his arm and grabs me by the waist, hoisting me up a few feet from the ground. I'm surprised he can pick me up, considering how skinny he seems.

I smile when he sets me down by the door. The knob is brass and cold when we put our hands to it. He nods, and we haul backwards, the door swinging wildly under our combined efforts. He grabs the edge before it swings back shut.

"After you, m'lady." He gives a cute half bow, and gestures into the dark.

"It's..." I start to say dark, but he pulls a flashlight out of his back pocket and shines it into the shadows. A smirk contorts his face.

The hall smells like soggy wood and rust when I stick my head in, and I'm pulled the rest of the way by an arm around my waist. The door shuts behind us with a gut wrenching thud; I feel trapped but it's not all horrible. I look up, and even in just a small bit of light his eyes still burn bright emerald green. It's amazing. He's to the side and behind me, and we silently take in the little bits we can as the small stream of light passes over the walls.

"Why does it stink so bad in here?" His face is so close to my temple I can feel his breath as he exhales sharply.

"A leak?" It's likely, but considering the weather has been abnormally dry all summer, I'm hesitant to fully commit to that theory.

He stops abruptly, and the beam of light drops to our feet. "Gross." Dried blood stains the floor under an abnormally large rat. The stain seems too big to have been made by the thing's body contents alone. When we were younger, Mabel used to sacrifice mice during one of her 'rituals'; maybe someone else in the neighborhood decided to take up 'witchcraft.' The spot could contain the blood of a dozen rats. I lean in closer to see if it's fresh. There is a slit down its front half, nearly splitting it in two, but the internal organs haven't been affected by gravity; it's all still tucked neatly away inside the abdomen.

It suddenly gives way, and I'm stumbling back as the shoe sized mammal turns itself inside out. My stomach twists, and threatens to mimic the rat.

"Sick!" He sounds almost excited, and not completely repulsed by the science class experiment that just happened at our feet. I hide in his shirt, sniffing the familiar cologne to calm my stomach.

"The basement is right over here." Changing the subject doesn't help, I'm still queasy from the blood smell and moist air.

A door creaks.

"What was that?" I take his hand and point the flashlight behind us but there's nothing.

"I didn't hear—" I shush him before he can finish and shine light toward the basement door. It's cracked even though when I left the other day I shut it behind me.

Maybe it's just my overactive imagination, but I could swear I see a tail slither away from the doorway into the room below. Not anything like a rat's tail. More like a slug. A pink, fleshy slug.

My hand is still on his, guiding the light toward the blackened basement doorway when we both hear it. Strange gurgles and wet foot falls echo through the tight space, pressing the sound onto me, and I'm heavy with panic. My feet can't carry me fast enough. As soon as I manage to push the door open again, I scramble across the sanctuary toward the exit.

"Brenna!" Niven is behind me, running along with me, but I can tell he wants me to slow down. He grabs my arm, spinning me around to face him, and we slam into the wall. The door beside us was my destination, but now I'm consumed with the thought of being shielded by a boy. Strange blends of emotions well up from my chest and heat my cheeks. When I look up he's protecting me; looking over his shoulder for signs of something following us. I can't will myself to move.

"I don't think there's anything down there." He turns to face me, and smiles. I have a sinking feeling that he's enjoying this. His smile feels gloating and evil.

"You're screwing with me aren't you?"

"Only if you want me to be." The way his eyebrow arches sends butterflies loose in my middle, all the air draining from my lungs. I'm not in the mood for games. I push him away and yank the door open.

"I'm sorry!" He grabs my hand again, but I slip through his fingers and down the hall. He calls for me, but stops just outside the doorway. Something tells me to wait and see what happens next, but gut instinct demands I leave. I turn, and keep my eyes on him. We stay like that for a long minute.

"There are rumors that—" He begins, but cuts himself off to stare at the monstrous door to his side; we've used it so much it's dust free, and gleaming dark mahogany in the sun.

"Yeah?" I insist. It's only another few seconds before my survival instincts win out over the butterflies that his messy hair generates, and I turn toward the exit.

"Rumors about something in the basement that eats men whole. Crushes their bones in its rows of steel-strong molars, and grows stronger by consuming their souls."

"Bull-shit." The words are just a typical social reaction, and I know it before I say it that I don't believe them. I saw something in that basement, even if my mind tells me to reject it as a delusion—just my overactive imagination again. It's a fact that I create unlikely scenarios that play out right in front of me, but what do I do when it's accompanied by such a strong physical reaction? Everything in my body is screaming to run away from this place, and when I look at Niven, he's so serious. "God, what am I saying? I just saw something. Let's just get out of here, real or not, whatever. I don't want to be eaten."

Niven doesn't move. "I can't go home."

"God, why not?" I'm losing it every second I stay, the memory of that *thing* in the other room gnawing at my mind.

He doesn't answer, just rubs his arm and heads back into the sanctuary. It's a few long seconds of deliberating—pacing back and forth, talking to myself—before I finally chase after him. The light is fading into evening and I can't stand the way it burns the room in orange; I hate the color orange. I take the stairs by two's and find Niven sprawled in the middle of the nearly black hardwood floor, bright light cuts across the balcony through the framing in the window, striping funny lines across his body.

"I only go home when I need to stock up on food," He says with his eyes closed, letting himself enjoy the sun's warmth.

"So you just let your parents worry," I say, "then you steal from them? It can't possibly be that bad where you live." Memories of the bruises, apologies, and pain come flooding into my heart, hardening my expression.

He pulls up his shirt, revealing a potato sized purple welt on his ribcage. The sight hits me like I've been punched too. The sun is dropping to the tree-line and the room turns a cooler hue, it calms any orange-rage I had still flowing in my mind. Goosebumps flood my skin, and my stomach sinks to my feet—feet that are barely holding me up as I walk to him. I fall to my knees by his side, and gently touch the raised skin on his side, he winces.

"What'd you do?"

"Stole food." His eyes are mocking, but his voice isn't playful anymore, and I understand completely.

"When did you get this?"

"Last night."

I let my finger trace the circular swollen area. I'm not sure why I do it, but he doesn't stop me. Everything is different all at once and I have to lie down to keep from falling I'm so light headed. I've never had anything nearly as big, or so purple, and it's sobering. My hand traces my cheekbone, where I was struck last, and I press down hard.

"Do you have anywhere to go?" I ask, after a long stretch

of silence.

"No." Doubt creeps into me at his quick response but I don't push him. My hand finds his, and our fingers weave together. He gives me a squeeze.

"We could run away."

"We barely know each other." I remind him. But even if we did, I'm not sure I could just leave everything behind. Mabel talks about it daily, and I've definitely thought about it, I just don't have a good enough plan yet. The way his fingers move in-between mine makes me wish more than anything that I could. I turn on my side to watch his face in the fading light.

"Brenna," He's whispering, but there are only the two of us, "When will you bring me your stories?" I wish he'd forgotten about those.

"Next time."

"Next time." He catches my eye out of the corner of his, sending a chill up my spine.

CHAPTER SEVEN

I'M IN THE balcony with Niven until the quietest hours of the morning talking about anything that comes to mind. Parents, siblings, the horrible things Mabel gets me into, and the people who blame me for things she's done.

"I need to go, I don't want..." I can't finish my thought, but I'm confident he understands. We're lying together watching the little bits of moonlight flutter in through the warped glass from the window. His fingers have been drawing spirals and figure eights on my arms for hours, making the surface of my body statically charged. "I wish the moon was full. I hate it when the night's pitch black." I wait, staring up at his serene face before I ask, "Draw the moon for me."

"Go home. Come back before it's full."

On the walk home, the sound of my shoes crunching gravel combined with the cold air leaves permanent goose bumps on my arms, and I can't figure out why I didn't bring his hoodie back to him. I make a mental note to return it to him as soon as possible. Halfway home, about the time I start seeing three dimensional shadows, I go from a slow walk to a hurried hop-jog, holding my arms tight to myself. I suddenly realize I'm perpetually frightened.

The moon, nearly gone tonight, streaks down my street in a perfectly straight line and I break into a run when my feet hit the light. My lungs burn as I haul myself into my bedroom window and collapse onto my mattress.

"You stink." Mabel makes snorting noises from across the room.

"I'll take a shower in the morning." I roll over and pass out, but it feels like only seconds before I'm awake again.

My pillow diffuses all the morning noises I make, when I hear a voice from the corner of the room. "I see you also crash into bed fully clothed."

I flip around and back up against the wall, staring at a wide-eyed, innocent Wyatt.

"Jesus, Wyatt." I rub my eyes and pull my shirt up from my elbow to place it back on my shoulder.

"So I was thinking…." His eyebrows pinch together and he looks down at his hands. "I can probably get you a job at the library."

"Can we talk after I get a shower?" I sniff my armpits, and my face automatically smashes into something unattractive. He shrugs, and I squeeze my eyes shut. "Come on."

I leave him at the bathroom counter, and threaten him with a plunger to the face if he gets pervy on me while I shower. "Just sit there and talk away."

"It's super easy, you just put the books back on the shelves. I know you can do that. And sometimes you have to read to kids if the librarian is sick."

The warm water is euphoric, and I'm only half paying attention to him. "I don't think I've ever been in the same room with a child."

I hear him picking things up and putting them back; he's snooping through our minimal amount of beauty products. A bottle of hand soap, a tube of toothpaste, and Mabel's stolen make-up that I don't touch.

Shampoo streams down my face, and I spit the small bit that gets in my mouth. "But I'm sure I can manage."

"Then we could hang out, after." He taps his fingers on the counter. "I've got some stuff I want to research, but it's kind of freaky being at the library alone at night."

"This is sounding pervy."

"Oh, shut up. You'd be scared in a dark room looking up old newspaper articles about hauntings and stuff. I just don't want to be alone." He pauses before he asks, "Do you think my brother died in that church?"

"I don't know." I spit water again and rub my palms into my face forcefully; I can't say I really do. Though, I'm pretty sure there is something in the basement of that damn place that could have eaten him. My fingers comb through my hair, and the water beads down my forehead and off my chin, while I try to enjoy the fresh, clean sensation. When it's wet, my hair dips down nearly to my belly button, and it takes forever to get all the shampoo out sometimes. It's slipping over my knuckles, and suddenly something is off.

I open my eyes, looking at my cupped hands that hold the bottom quarter of my hair, to find it's no longer split ends staring back at me—it's snake heads. Black, scaly, and swaying upright in my palm. They watch me intently as I process my new status as Medusa of Hannigan, KY. I can't scream. Wyatt would wonder why I'm flailing in the shower for no reason, because I'm only dreaming. Just another vivid product of my broken head.

The muscles under their cold skin swell as they breathe, and a whimper escapes from my nose at the sensation. Their red tongues snap out at me in slow motion and I start to hyperventilate, unable to control myself for much longer. They slither up my arm onto my shoulder and my hair moves with them. I hold back the revulsion as best I can, though vomiting right now could get Wyatt to leave before I start screaming.

"Are you almost done?" He asks, and my physically attached pets hiss loudly in his direction. "What the hell?"

"Get out!" My voice finally escapes my throat, and soon after I'm screaming; screaming and thrashing my arms at my own head to make it stop. None of it is real.

It isn't real.

Stop it!

I drop to my knees, letting my hair fall into a veil around me and find the reptiles have vanished. The grip I have on the soap holder turns my knuckles white, and I shake my hands to get rid of the ache. The hand pain is replaced by overwhelming embarrassment as I try to come up with an excuse for my behavior. Hopefully he didn't run straight out the front door after that crazy episode. I step out of the tub onto my dirty clothes, and grab a big bath towel from the shelf beside the shower stall.

"Wyatt?" My arms grip the terry cloth, keeping it wrapped tightly around me, as I peer into my bedroom for my only friend in the world. He's sitting on Mabel's bed, cross-legged, and stares at me, obviously unnerved.

"Roach," I say.

His eyes roll back into his head and he flops onto the mattress, letting loose all the fear he was holding onto. "I thought you had snakes in the shower with you or something!"

I laugh nervously, unsure if I had made those sounds or if there had really been snakes attached to the ends of my hair. I sweep it all to one side, over my shoulder, to double check. The wet strands drip down my back and arm, sending a wild shiver through my body. "Turn around."

Clothes are everywhere, making it difficult to find what I need. Luckily, I have clean underwear in the dresser under the window, and cover my most embarrassing bits quickly. A pair of shorts show up by my bed, and I find a loose purple shirt I wore a few days ago under my pillow. I sniff it before throwing it over my head. I throw one of Mabel's shoes in his direction when I'm done.

"You could have just said, done." He flings the shoe back at me with a chuckle.

"So can I work all day, every day?" I'm serious, but I smirk like I'm joking when Wyatt's face turns downward. I know he's seen the bruises. There is a limit to how long shorts can be before it looks suspicious, not to mention wearing long sleeve shirts in a hot school gym is over the top weird. He grabbed my arm once during class, just to test a theory.

"You can work as often as you're scheduled, and hang out with me after to help with this research."

"Do you get to be my guide, or trainer, or something?" I ask.

He smile. "You'll be on all my shifts for a week, at least. Then you can ask for a change once you're sick of me."

"What if I'm already sick of you?" I toss a pillow at him and he catches it.

"Hey, you're the one who said you'd shovel horse shit into a bucket, am I worse than that?" I smirk and teeter my hand, debating it in my head playfully—he hits me right in the face with the pillow.

"Baby Brenna!" Mabel sings my name across the house and terror wells up inside of me, making me frantic to get Wyatt out without a scene.

"There you are." She slides into the room and ruffles my hair. "When are you going to get some girlfriends, baby sister?"

Her arms are folded as she stares Wyatt down.

I shift my weight from one leg to the other before smoothing my hair back down. It's already drying frizzy in the humid air of the house. "Wyatt got me a job. We have to leave."

I jerk my head in the direction of the bedroom door, begging him to get up as my sister peruses her closet, flipping shirts to one side like she's bored. He doesn't move, just shrugs his shoulders and makes a stupid boy face. That stupid boy face I see every time she's around a stupid boy; Wide-eyed, in awe of her. My shoes are at the door, so I grab them as I leave. He deserves everything he gets for not following me. I tried to get him out, but he just didn't get it.

"Brenna, stop." Mabel grabs my elbow as I reach the back door. Her confidence is shrinking, and her eyes are pleading me to listen, but I just don't want to hear it anymore.

"Like you do?" My vision falls to the floor, right where Danny nearly scalped me. "Like you stop? I can when you can."

"Just listen," She says, begging me to sit down at the table. Wyatt appears out of the shadows at the doorway, and I take the chance to use him as an escape.

"I can't. We need to leave." I rip my arm out of her hand. "I'll see you later."

My feet slide around inside my shoes as I bound down the back steps, and I'm angry I forgot socks. The heat makes them sweat, and the sweat makes them slide, and I can't stop thinking about my stupid sister and what she could possibly need to tell me so bad. I'm tired of her problems. I'd have no problems if I didn't have her problems.

"When do I get my first paycheck?" I say, to break the silence we've been in since we left the house. His hands are stuffed into his pants pockets, and he's rolling something around between his fingers; he doesn't answer me.

"Why don't you two get along?" He asks, keeping his eyes on the road.

"Because, one, she's a psychotic bitch." I kick a rock with all the anger I'm holding onto. I'd hoped it would make me feel better, but it doesn't.

"But she's you're sister." He's insistent, confused with why I would hate my blood relative so much.

"And two, she doesn't love me." I say, and it's the only thing I know to be true in my life. She doesn't love me. If she loved me she wouldn't get me into situations that could kill me. "If she loved me she would have protected me."

I don't know what I mean by that, and I didn't mean to say it, but my thoughts are so deafeningly loud lately that I can't discern them from speech at times. I chance a look at him, and he's still fondling something in his pocket. Probably another bone or fossil.

"Here." He takes it out and it's the fossil of the many legged bug I saw on his shelf at his house. "I saw you looking at it and thought you might like it."

I don't really like it, but I know I shouldn't tell him that.

I take it and put it in my pocket.

"My brother used to take me 'stuff hunting'." He stops at the end of the street, and kicks some long grass around with his foot. "We used to find bones, fossils, teeth, coins…" He lets his voice trail off as he reaches down to pick up a feather. It's red and beautiful, and I selfishly wish he'd give that to me instead of the weird rock.

He smiles. "I just can't stop looking for stuff. I was so little, I barely remember him, but I remember when he'd take me to hunt for things."

"At least you have something nice to remember him by, I just have—" He cuts me off.

"You just have every day." His eyes go right through me, and I'm nervous for my soul, he seems to be condemning it to hell with his stare.

A warm wave of rage rises up in my chest. "Stop comparing our lives. It won't bring him back and you can't make my life better by pretending I'm overreacting. You don't know her."

He scowls for a split second before we continue walking. I don't mean to be harsh, but he can't make me feel bad for saying it.

"Here." He shoves the feather at me as we hit the sidewalk.

"Thanks."

We walk silently and slowly toward the library, when a thought comes out urgently. "I need job stuff, don't I? Birth certificate and everything?" I turn around, and rake my hand through my hair. I don't want to see her again, not after I just blew her off. Not after Wyatt tried to set me on fire with his eyes for hating her so much.

"Yeah, I guess you do." He turns around with me, but doesn't start back toward the house.

"Why don't I just meet you there?" I ask.

He shrugs and turns. His shoulders are slumped, and I can't help the way my stomach tightens at the sight of him, knowing I only perpetuate his sadness with my seemingly childish sibling rivalry. But he doesn't know us, he barely knows me.

"Work, paycheck, get out of town. Work, paycheck, get out of town..." I repeat to myself as I slide around the outside of the house, avoiding contact with Mabel at all costs. The front of the house has untrimmed, dying rose bushes that scrape at my legs as I creep toward the window to Dad's room. Doors slam, and Mabel lets out a scream of frustration while stomping through the house. I roll my eyes, wondering what she could possibly be so angry about.

"All for nothing!" Her words drift out of the open window, just after a tiny shimmering speck sails through the air overhead. I watch it land in the hedge line that separates our house from the one next door.

"Shit!" She screams it over and over again under her breath as she searches the room for whatever she threw. She must not know it went sailing through the window like a freed bird. I listen as she holds back sobs in a familiar way, and in my mind I can see her stretching her face taut, from her nose to her ears with her palms, like she often does. I wonder, for a brief moment, if that's why she's wrinkling by her eyes already.

I peek up at the window and make a dash for the bright green shrubs, digging quietly in the dense branches where I saw the shiny object land. My hand finds a key ring, and when I pull it out I'm staring at a pair of funny looking gold keys. I run back to the side of the house and hear her pushing both the window panes upwards so she can climb out. Finally, I have something, even if I don't know what it means. I have something to possibly get her to leave me alone. I take off toward the church.

CHAPTER EIGHT

"WHAT TOOK YOU so long?" Wyatt asks when I finally make it to the library.

Oh, I just stole some keys from Mabel, and gave them to my secret-maybe-someday-boyfriend who camps out inside an abandoned church where your brother may or may not have died. Just that.

"I couldn't find where he keeps the files." I say as I sit down across from him. It's partially the truth. It did take a while to find the folder stuffed inside Dad's closet that held my job-getting informational documents.

We're surrounded by towering shelves of books in a little circle of tables and chairs. Bright florescent lights flicker ever so slightly overhead, and an air conditioner thumps and hums loudly off in the corner. I couldn't concentrate on reading something here if I had a gun to my head.

"Here." He slides a few sheets of paper across the white

laminate table toward me, and one catches the air, floating above us like a gymnast. I grab a pen from the pile Wyatt has, and start filling out the easy things. Name, birthday.

"I forgot," he says as he peers over at the date on the paper. "We're twins."

I smile, worried he was going to keep the sour face all afternoon. His expression is less of a sneer, but not yet a smile. At least it's something.

He's writing in a notebook, and I wonder if it's a story. He catches me staring, probably because I'm not writing anymore, and turns the notebook to face me.

"Lists of hauntings in the state, and surrounding states. I can't find anything about that haunted church." He flips the page and points to the long list of names. "This isn't everyone, but close to all the priests who preform, or have performed, exorcisms in the area. Just in case they know something."

The word exorcism sends chills up my back, cold reaper's fingers tickling my spine. The rituals Mabel did, and the Ouija boards we used seem childish in comparison. But who's to say any of it's real? Not that I'm a good judge anymore, with my possible mental instability.

"Are you really going to make me stay late to help you with this?"

"Why?" He smirks. "Are you scared?"

"Yes," I say, honestly. What I don't say is how Mabel used to do séances when we were in middle school, swearing she could contact mom, but only ended up scaring me into insomnia. She'd surround us with candles and tell me to focus, to not think of anything but the crazy brown curls that sprang from our mother's head—something I've only seen in a picture. I'd end up dizzy and crying, hugging the pillow that's embroidered with her name. I found it in the closet one time when I was hiding from dad. Blackness would seep into my vision, taking me away to a dream filled with ghosts and demons. She'd tell me later, when I woke up, that I was channeling Mom's spirit and she wanted us to find her. I'd ask if that meant she was dead, but Mabel would just ignore me.

"It's not so bad," he says, going back to his notebook and a phone book. "I haven't found anything that wasn't easily explained away. It's going to be hard to prove he's not a runaway." He picks up another notebook from the floor beside him, and flips a page open to a torn post-it.

"There was a 'haunting' a few miles outside of Lexington, but it was just an automatic light from a cell tower combined with a really punctual train on Thursdays." He looks sternly at his writing, possibly willing it to be more interesting, instead of a big disappointment.

"So, is this your hobby then?" I ask, itching to have a notebook of my own. I'd describe the way his eyes show everything he's feeling like a billboard: scared, frustrated, lost, but also determined. He's chewing on his cheek as he doodles in the margins of the paper.

He hands me another paper, a short test on classifications and alphabetizing, that I breeze through without a problem.

Something I'm good at, finally.

"I can't really find anything about the church on 12th street." He chews on his other cheek, probably gritting his teeth too, grinding them to numb the pain of not knowing what happened to his brother.

"St. Dymphna Catholic Church." I say, pompously, and mostly to myself, but Wyatt makes a choking noise.

"What?" His hands are flat on the table as he stares, wide-eyed at me like I've scared him. His body is tense and electric with excitement.

"Stop it," I say, "You look like a jumpy puppy."

"Why does the plaque out front say, 'Our Lady of Peace'?"

"Vandalism?" It isn't a stretch. There isn't much to do in this town but drink, or hit your kids. At least that's been my personal experience. I actually don't know why they changed the name. "Maybe they were trying a positive approach to attract new members. My dad has always called it St. Dymphna."

"Well that changes a lot, I've only been looking up the name from the sign, if something happened there a long time ago it wouldn't be under, 'Our Lady of Peace.'" He grabs his notebooks and my papers from the table, placing them to his chest as he stands.

"Where do I start?" I ask, standing and sweeping my hair over my other shoulder.

He points to a cart overflowing with books the size of my

head. "Put away the large print."

He takes off toward the office, and I'm left with my thoughts and the rumble of air conditioning vents.

The muscles in my shoulders have never been so sore—never been used this often or in this manner. Straining to slip cumbersome books into tiny spaces well above my head proves to be a much more strenuous task than I'd anticipated. I'm too lazy to look for a step ladder, or ask for one, so I spend some of the time quietly climbing shelves to reach the top racks.

A huge historical fiction novel, about Amish women behaving like the Orange county housewives (I had to flip through it!), is being difficult—to say the least—putting me up two shelves, balancing horribly with both hands above my head. Of course, Wyatt chooses just this moment to sneak up on me.

"Get the ladder." He tilts his head angrily. I'm an insurance liability, I know, but I just want to get into a rhythm and forget about things for a while. Maybe that's what Wyatt means about reading for a distraction. Something to keep from thinking about the reality that rips at your skin. Erasing all the people that burn away your layers until you feel raw and sticky, tender to the touch.

I hop down. "Sorry. I'm a climber."

"Just…" He sighs, and shakes his head. "Just get the step ladder thing if you can't reach. I'll get my ass handed to me if they see you. They as in Janet, the librarian who apparently hates your mom."

Great, my mother isn't even a part of my life, but she can still leave her stamp on everything in town. Just like my sister. "Fine." I can't help how my jaw muscles contract. She doesn't even know me, she's never even seen me that I know of.

"Don't worry about it." Wyatt kicks the toe of my sneaker and hands me a badge, name and all. Brenna Bowman, Page.

"That was fast."

"I am the Hannigan library. Computers, printers, scheduling... you name it, I can do it. I'm a freaking rock star here; a book labyrinth deity."

I laugh. "Oh my god, should I throw my panties?"

His face flushes red, but he smirks with a nod. "It happens all the time."

The sun is starting to dip out of sight, meaning the library will be closing to the public soon. I'm not sure how excited I am to sit in drafty halls of words, researching ghosts and demons in the dark, but if it keeps me from having to go home it can't be that bad.

"Do you want to hang out here or come to the break room with me? I have a box of Little Debbie's." He totes the last part like it's a huge selling point, and it totally is.

"Um, why didn't you say something earlier? Yes, definitely, yes."

"It's past the bathrooms," he says, as he backs up with the empty book cart. "I'm going to lock up."

The library really is a sort of labyrinth, and I get lost twice before I find the bathrooms. As I drag my hand along the wall—a stupid habit—I remember the way blood pooled in my hand last time and clutch it to my chest. At the end of the hallway is a plain metal door labeled 'Office', and is propped slightly open. The place is flooded in black, even when I push the door wider into the room. It's silent and still as I run my hand along the inside wall searching for the light switch. Something sharp slices hot into my skin. I rip my hand back out of the room, choking on air in surprise. My teeth press into my jaw as I bite through a scream and put pressure to my hand. The scream I suppress rolls out of my nose as a deep groan instead.

"What happened?" Wyatt sprints down the hall at full speed, and spins around me into doorway to hit the switch sending the darkness into the corners of the room. He grabs my hand and opens my palm to face him. Nothing.

"I..." Words escape me. I felt a razor burn straight through my flesh, I know it.

"Did the switch shock you?" He flips it a few times. Off, on, off, on, off.

I hesitate, staring at the hand that should be half open. "Yeah, it shocked me."

"Well." He claps his hands together. "Let's figure this church place out. I keep imagining it's some entrance to an underground society that my brother pledged to, like a fraternity." That he's not really dead, is what he doesn't say.

The skin on my palm prickles and stings as I take a seat.

"That would be cool, can my unicorns come with us when we infiltrate their secret hideout?" The table is filled with stacks of books.

He grunts as he sits, and bumps the table, sending two heavy books into my lap. Pain radiates down my legs, tickling my toes before coming back up to settle in my stomach as a nauseating wave. "Sorry."

I place the creepy occult books back on the table, trying hard not to let my hands linger on the binding. A shiver courses down my back at the macabre images that flash in my mind.

"I guess I should just get used to you, huh?" He flips open his notebook to an orange post-it, and starts crossing out lines.

"I don't know. I just..." I give up trying to explain what I am. "Why are you crossing those out?"

"They are priests and hauntings that came up in searches for 'Our Lady of Peace', and I think we're going to have more luck with the old name."

The floor in the office is laminate tiles, they are a blue wavy pattern that changes very little throughout the room. I kick off my shoes under the table, and sit cross legged in my chair with my knees peeking out of the arm rest squares. I consider the black cover of the book in front of me, too afraid to even read the title.

I'm afraid of everything. Everything not grounded in reality, really. Murderers, natural disasters, or accidental deaths—the things that should scare me—aren't anything I even flinch about. But show me a picture of a black mark in the corner of a room, and claim it's a ghost, you'll quickly have a blubbering mess of a girl. Scratch the wall as we walk down a silent hallway, and watch my jump sky high. It's mortifying at times. Like now, when I can't even open a book.

"That's a good one. Talks about demon persuasion and manipulation."

I swallow hard as I split the book in half, slamming the cover onto the table. This might not be better than being at home. I flip through pages and pages of what seems like gibberish, but after a while figure out it's chants in Latin. The block quotes of italics should have tipped me off, but the dread of turning the page to an image of someone contorted in spine severing angles has me tuned out entirely. Pages and pages of rituals and chants, but nothing that would explain seeing a fleshy tail in a basement.

"We need something to tell us about the man-swallowing, bone eater thing that lives in the basement. Where's the book on that?" The pages flit though the air as I snap them from side to side, scanning multiple instances of 'Dei iudicium', 'Deus tecum' and 'caelitus mihi vires' for anything about flesh gnawing demons.

"What are you talking about?"

"The urban legend? The thing that swallows men whole and crushes their bones in its massive teeth and lives off their souls…" I say this like he should know it, but I just learned about it a day ago from a boy who lives in the church with it.

It's probably his pet. I laugh to myself, and Wyatt just stares.

"I've got to start mental screenings on my friends."

"Come on," I say, slamming my hands down on the book. "I'm just feeling cookie teased. Where's my food?" I'm not crazy, just interesting.

He tosses an individually wrapped oatmeal crème sandwich my way, and I nearly inhale it, calming my instincts only when I think of how ladies should eat—what I'm doing isn't anything close.

"So, should we Google Bone-eater?"

"And bone eating demon, soul sucking incubus, bone crushing monster," I say. "You have to cover all your bases."

I follow him to the row of computers in the back of the labyrinth, and pull a chair around to sit beside him. He clicks and types, then we sit motionless for a while, staring at a little centered box on the screen.

"Bone eating demon." I whisper.

"Baigujing?" He clicks on the second result, and reads out loud about a character from a super old Chinese novel.

"I doubt it."

"Still." He writes notes on a little legal pad about the tricky, lying demon.

He scans a few more results, of demon bone earring listings, before sighing.

I pinch his arm. "Flesh eating demon."

He types quickly and clicks the first link, a list of demons. We read, our heads close together, inches from the screen, about Banshees and Furies before he stops at Pishacha.

"What's that?"

"A flesh eating demon that's grotesque and has bulging eyes." It also possesses humans, and alters their thoughts.

"Did you see its eyes?" I ask.

"I didn't see anything, I just have a gut feeling that—" I cut him off by dropping my head to the desk. A gut feeling?

"I thought you knew something! You didn't see anything at all?" I yell louder than I mean to.

"Stop, okay?" He pushes back from the desk, scraping the chair across the floor in a hideous screech.

"Well, we don't even know what we're looking for. Did something eat your brother? Did he really join a secret society? Did he ever even step foot inside that church?"

"He did." He snaps. "I followed him the night he disappeared. I just can't remember anything else about that night."

"So what's the next step then?" I scoot my chair in front of the keyboard and type, 'St. Dymphna Catholic Church' and come up with a few churches, but nothing in the area.

"Maybe we should just go in the church and look around?"

I panic. Niven needs to say hidden from his father. "Yeah, and then when we get in there we can split up to look for clues."

Behind me, he kicks the chair and I cringe knowing this isn't the best time to wield my sarcasm sword, but he's too curious. He kicks it again, and memories of my dad throwing dishes flash in my closed eyelids. I'm squeezing them shut, willing myself not to shake—to keep breathing. I need to stay, not run.

"What am I supposed to do?" He pleads in a low, menacing voice. "Am I just supposed to let this go and let the recurring dreams keep me up at night? Let the gut wrenching guilt eat at me until I'm a shell of a person? Huh?"

I wince as he walks closer with each question, until he's right beside me.

"I'm sorry." It comes out shallow and pathetic. I swallow and run my tongue along my dry lips.

"Yeah."

"Wyatt…" I turn in my chair to look at him cautiously. He's got his hands stuffed in his pockets, and his shoulders slump in embarrassment. This time it's louder. "I'm sorry."

"I know," he says. "Me too."

He pulls the chair up next to me, and we stare at a fresh search screen. "What ever happened to those guys that were chasing you?"

"I don't know."

CHAPTER NINE

THERE'S NO MOON light to bathe in as I walk past the broken gate toward my fawn colored shack of a house. The streetlight only illuminates the front half of the property, causing temporary blindness once I turn the corner to the back steps. I hesitantly press finger tips to the siding for guidance in the dark. The door is unlocked—no need for the key under the mat—so I creep inside, trying not to wake him. I left a note about having a job; he better be proud.

I flip the switch and cringe in the bright orange that blankets the room, the florescent strip above my head flickers. Half of the fixture has been faulty for months, blinking every now and then, trying to warn us of its impending death. Slowly, I shut the door, twisting the knob after it's closed to keep as silent as possible.

The light flutters once, twice, then shorts out, sparking before it kills the breaker with it. I flip the hall switch, but nothing happens. I take in a lung full of air to help ease my growing fear, but goose bumps rush down my arms and up my legs as I stagger in the black hallway, feeling for the closet door that has the breaker box. Fluffy coats and boxes crowd me as I maneuver around them toward the metal door that holds the little dams of power. The plastic rectangles are all facing the same direction, a straight line down both sides. Something grazes my arm in the darkness. I shake my arm violently and hit the panel door, scraping the back of my hand. "Damn it."

There's a big switch at the top of the panel, but I don't know if it's supposed to be flipped in the same direction as the others or not. I test it, and a gold strip forms at the bottom of the door from the hall light turning on. I shut the panel and shimmy out of the closet, closing the door behind me.

Dad must be out at the bar, being social, surprisingly. But I still don't want to be visible when he gets home. Pretending to be asleep is my specialty. Instead of going to my room I'm lured back the way I came; a voice telling me to check the locks. I expect the kitchen light is done for, but something else is amiss. When I round the corner the back door is wide open, letting the cold slip in uninvited. Tension floats in the air between me and the opening. I push past it to slam the door and lock it, but not quickly enough. I catch a shadow in the backyard at the fence line, lurking. The frame shakes with my fear-filled strength, and I smash my face to the half window, pushing the aluminum blinds to the side.

No shadow. Just my crazy. I hit my temple. My stupid

head.

I turn the deadbolt.

My hand instinctively rubs the tickle on the back of my neck as I head into our bedroom. It turns into frantic scratching before I slam my bedroom door shut, and I let out a shaky breath. Home shouldn't be this scary, it's where I should feel safe. Even the walls are trying to get to me. Tiny nails, digging from the other side of the drywall, have me snapping my head all around, searching for the mouse or bird trying to get out. It stops for a split second each time I turn around.

Damn Wyatt. Damn him and his creepy research, and his creepy story.

The scratching gets louder, scraping and shifting incessantly, until I kick over a pile of my clothes in the corner where the sound seems to originate. It stops, and there's nothing coming out of the walls, or the floor, thankfully. The only oddity is a gray stain on the laminate wood that I don't remember being there before. I reach down to check the clothes for dampness, but they're dry.

The door slams, jolting my body upright. I hit the light, and collide with my mattress, flying the blanket behind me like a cape. I calm my breathing, and slow my heart to as steady a rate as I can, before Mabel bursts through the door.

"We should go shopping tomorrow, baby sister. Mama is loaded." She's tipsy, if not drunk, and I don't want to be seen with her, ever. My eyes don't even flutter; never betraying me like my sister would.

"Are you seriously asleep at barely midnight, you fruit-cake?" She shakes me but I just lay limp, like I'm so far gone I can't be roused for anything. I listen as she stifles giggles, and rummages around in her purse for something. Some more giggles escape her before I hear the familiar click of a BIC. Snap, snap, snap. Giggles turn into snorts, and I'm sure she's drunk.

"Fire!" She shakes me again. Not for anything, even fire. My back feels warm and there's an odor in the air that I can't place. Plastic, or skin.

It's hair. My hair.

I swallow. Nothing, not even my hair on fire. She's not worth it.

"Oh my god!" She beats me with her bare hands. "Oh my god, Brenna, just…just…" She breathes slower and sits down on the mattress. "Just, oh my god." Her arm snakes around my waist as she kisses, what I assume is, my fried hair, and breathes an apology. She pats my back, and I listen to her feet thump down the hall toward the bathroom. Water fills the pipes in the wall with rushing squeals and hums as I reach for the back of my head to assess the damage. There's a chunk of sticky at the end but nothing life changing.

Muffled sounds echo in the hall, tapping at the door, teasing me with snippets of the song my sister is singing to herself in the bathtub. An old song our dad used to sing around us when we were kids, something about the devil's eyes.

I sit up, and try to finger comb the gross out of my tangled curls. She's still singing about fire and smiles, but her voice is becoming distant. The knot won't come out, and it's hurting my scalp more each time I pick at it. I don't hear her finish the song. I wait for it.

All I hear is water splashing.

And a choking, painful gasp for air so loud I hear it right through the closed door.

I stumble and reach for the knob, barely catching myself before slamming into the floor. The splashing stopped, but the gurgling and sputtering that replaces it is so much worse. I spin into the room, sliding on the tiny checkered tiles, and dive into the black water, cradling Mabel's head as it surfaces.

Her eyes are black holes, empty sockets with no end, and her mouth twists up in a smile as she lets water seep out and run down its corners. Her hair is dull gray and matted, sticking to my skin like leeches. The ice cold water stings my flesh, but I can't let her go. Ambient light from the back door's flood lamp trickles in the window, turning the surface of the water reflective as it ripples around my arms. She spits a stream of shimmering liquid into the air and I jump back in surprise, hitting the cabinet with painful force. She's floating now.

"Mabel!" I go back toward her, but she starts speaking. Water pours in and out of her mouth as she chants in a language I don't recognize. I go for the tub again, this time to pull the plug but I stop short, watching the water roll in tiny circles curiously.

I fall back against the cabinet again. Dark, scaly talons

ooze over the edge toward me. Slowly and deliberately they slide down the side of the tub, like an overflowing jar of ink, and I crawl on my back across the floor, keeping an eye on the claws that extend from the long, rough fingers. I scramble to my feet, launching myself out into the black dark behind the house, toward a place I can feel safe again.

I run into the middle of the street disoriented and sweating, debating where to go at midnight that could possibly help calm my raging mind. I turn to the right, toward Wyatt and the library, but a pair of glowing eyes in the fence line ahead sends me scrambling in the opposite direction, slipping on the alleyway's gravel floor.

My head is vibrating and ringing so loud I'm surprised when I see the steeple in the distance; my distress hasn't rendered me completely confused and lost. At some point I started crying, and now I can't stop the tears. I left her. She could be dead, floating, bloated in the tub at home, alone. And I left her. I stop at the steps leading up to the boarded front door, and watch the shadows of the trees dance across the wood, stone, and brick that compose the towering building I'll find refuge in.

The window around the side is shut, like usual, but it's harder to open than it was before. I stretch tall, wiggling my fingers into the tiny gap between the two framed panes of glass and wonder if Niven fixed it and locked himself in.

Wind rustles the bushes by the tree line and I recoil, holding my hands to my chest. Nothing in the dark resembles what it is in the light, so I refuse to acknowledge the werewolf sized shadow that breathes with the wind. Especially since my eyes can't be trusted. The cold bricks freeze my back as I flatten against them, watching the shape shift and stretch into an upright position. My fingernails dig into my palms, making marks from the force of my grip.

Fingers from above brush my cheek. "Shhh," he whispers, "Don't scream."

I hit his arm with a gasp, turning around and falling into an overgrown circle of tall grasses. "Don't do that."

He helps me into the window—nice, even though I don't need it—letting his hand linger in mine as I close the window behind us. He squeezes my hand. "Are you cold?"

My body is shaking uncontrollably, and it's not from being cold. "I don't know what's going on. I keep seeing things, and it's getting worse. These..." I don't want to use the word.

"Hallucinations?" I cringe at the ease in his voice, his curious tone grates on my ears. It's not a novelty to me.

"Come here." He pulls me into a hug, but I'm distracted by the way his shadow hits the floor. It's long and curved, towering over my own by several feet, hunched forward in an inhuman way. I'm shivering again, and he glances at the floor where I'm staring. I can feel his smile spreading on my forehead as he turns us—our own strange, abandoned building prom night—and our shadows twist, alternating between being tall and short. I don't understand the physics of it, but I assume it has something to do with the warped window panes that the street light shines through. It's nothing to worry about.

"My sister may have drowned in the bathtub tonight." I say as we continue our slow dance, accompanied by decor of busted pipes jetting out from the wall and chirping cicadas as a soundtrack.

His breathing is even and steady, such a contrast from my own hiccupping sobs. "I doubt it."

"There was someone outside my house tonight, or maybe there wasn't. I'm not sure about anything anymore." Except that everything seems to be spiraling out of control, just as I got a job—right when I start making progress on getting the hell out.

"Probably just more..." I tense in anticipation of the word and he stops short, letting it be.

He's wearing a t-shirt and khakis making me feel under dressed in my ratted, cut off jean shorts. My loose combat boots—that I grabbed while running out the back door—are difficult to dance in, so I step back when he tries to spin me. I stare at the floor, embarrassed at my lack of focus. I just can't take the feeling that I left my sister to die.

"Just shake it out." He wiggles my arms, then twirls me easily.

"It's just not a good time to dance."

"Is it a good time for presents?"

I look up at his eyes searching behind them for a hint of what he's talking about, but they're unyielding. He smirks.

He leads me into the sanctuary, and goes backwards up the stairs, holding both my hands in his. "Close your eyes."

"I don't really want to do that." I stop, but he holds tight to my hands.

"I promise you'll like it." He grins, stepping down to my level, easing his face into my personal space bubble.

"Just don't tell me to imagine anything, please."

"You won't have to." He pulls on my hand. "You'll see it the same as I do."

We turn the corner at the top, and I don't know how to process what's in front of me. The huge window that sits above the front door of the church is massive, nearly from floor to ceiling in the balcony, and he's covered it in papers. But it's not just papers, it's drawings. They're negatives; black to darken what shouldn't be seen instead of the color being the illustration on the white blankness of the paper. They are all connected by tiny squares of clear tape to form one giant picture. It's the moon shining cold, white light down into the room.

"You asked me to draw you the moon," He whispers from behind me.

"I always miss the moon when it's gone."

"Drawing it made me miss you." His breathe is warm on my temple, sending electric current down my arms. I'm supercharged and hugging myself. Should let myself feel anything for him when I may just leave town? What happens then? I close my eyes at the feeling of someone caring enough to miss me, and let it go when I realize he'll just end up hating me when I disappear.

"Don't miss me." I side step his looming presence, and rub my arms at the chilly balcony air. "I won't be around for long."

"Where are you going?" He comes toward me, cautiously. When I don't retreat, he invades my bubble completely, snaking his hands behind my arms and down to my palms, linking his fingers in mine.

"Getting out of town as soon as I have some cash."

"My offer still stands." He draws lines with his thumbs under my shirt on the bare skin of my hip. They are searing, and boil the blood underneath. I can't catch my breath.

"You'd just leave everything and follow me?"

"You'd just leave everything and let me?"

It strikes me harder than I would have imagined. I sink into his chest, thinking about Mabel's cold body floating in the bathtub. No matter how often I find myself hating what she does, I can't stop loving her. Maybe in another life I would be Wyatt, unable to look past the loss of my sister to continue my life. Instead, I stand in illustrated moonlight, wondering how I can be so cold.

CHAPTER TEN

I WAKE UP groggy and cranky from too many late nights. I rub my eyes to help them become less glued together, but it doesn't help. The house is quiet, save the incessant drip from the bathtub—a reminder of the crazy that's lingering somewhere in the back of my head.

There is one can left in the cardboard drink case on the counter. I don't bother to throw away the box since the trash can is already overflowing, and there aren't any bags left under the sink. I'll have to go shopping. Caffeine helps, but the effects of the generic lemon-lime soda are delayed, and the fact, that it's warm doesn't give me much of a reason to put a pep in my step. Mabel isn't home, and I assume she left after getting dad off to work because he's nowhere to be found. She wasn't in the bathtub when I reluctantly came home last night, so my imagining it is looking like the most likely scenario.

The house feels alive—it breathes in and makes me claustrophobic. I crush the can in my hand to lessen my growing anxiety, but it doesn't help, just scrapes at my hand without breaking skin. I dress quickly and hit the street, hoping to clock in early at the library. I need to add to my get-out-of-town fund. After checking for the key under the mat, I lock the back door then double check it just in case. I put the key in my pocket instead of out in the open; the creeper in the back yard put my self-preservation mode on high.

The newly sun-kissed grass sparkles with dew, and I have to restrain myself because I want to roll in it. It's already hot—being late August and all—making me slightly crazy with the anticipation of being sticky and uncomfortable. At least the library is air-conditioned.

When I get to the compound-like brick building, I'm struck by how early it actually is. The library won't open for another couple hours today. Something shiny flickers through the glass doors, calling me with a force I can't ignore. I check my surroundings for suspicious figures, but feel silly as stomp up to the cold clear wall to peer inside. Wyatt's head is poking out from behind a shelf looking eerily unconscious, or more possibly dead.

Instinct takes control, and I slap my hands to the glass in hopes of rousing him. I bang and yell his name, internally begging him to not be dead. I shake the door handles with every ounce of energy I have, but it isn't working, he's still immobile.

I stop—hesitate—what if I'm imagining this? I slide down

the barrier that's keeping me from my friend, angry that I can't keep reality and fantasy in check lately. Pulling my hair helps me focus sometimes, but today it's just painful, and I have to stop myself before I pull out chunks. Focus. I will myself to remember it's not real. Except when I glance over my shoulder he's still limp and lifeless, slowly killing my sanity.

I'm frantic as I run a circle around the building, looking for a way to get in. Faded bricks cut corners and stretch out in front of me. They're framed with random hedges, and trees I have to dodge. At the opposite side, there's an access door that I remember seeing on the way to the office. I check the knob, and it turns easily. My heart leaps into my throat, and my feet pound echoes into the narrow hallway as I sprint toward the front of the library.

When I finally reach his motionless body, I kneel beside him, tears streaming down my cheeks. "Wyatt, wake up. Please."

I'm pleading, shaking him viciously when he stirs. "Stop it."

I push him over, hard. "You were just asleep?"

"I guess I fell asleep reading this book on hypnosis. Irony?" He rubs his head and sits up. "I was up until…" He looks around for a clock to decide. "I don't even know when, looking at old newspapers on the Kodak."

"The what?"

He wipes drool residue from the corner of his mouth, then stands with a groan. "The ancient monster machine in the room with all the filing cabinets. There are drawers, and drawers of this microfilm stuff that has super old newspapers on it."

I take a deep breath, expelling the tightness from my chest, and try to calm my thoughts enough to concentrate. "What are you looking for?"

"Anything about my brother and his friends going missing. It was about eight years ago, he was sixteen." His eyes take on a glossy appearance as he scratches the side of his face in thought. He's consumed.

Trying not to feed into his obsession, I change the subject. "Should we clean up or anything? Do you need to go home for a shower?"

He looks down at his wrinkled khaki shorts, bulging on one side with *found stuff*, and flattens his black shirt before shrugging with a grunt. He's a mess. I'm guessing not too much different than his mother; hiding from her grief in cheap entertainment.

I pick up the book on hypnosis. "Do you think this would work?" I flip through the pages, shaking my head that I'd consider indulging him. The pages fly by, and a title hits my subconscious like a brick through a window, How to eliminate negative hallucinations through self-induced imagery. I scan the paragraphs of what I would consider nonsense any other day, and absorb ever word of it. Maybe I could help myself through helping Wyatt.

The day drags on—a long stretch of road in front of me on a

hot afternoon—miserable, and repetitive. The only bright spot is the handful of times I catch a scent of thick paper and remember Niven's drawings—and his eyes. It's weird to think he may be camping out in a murder scene hotel, and I wonder if he knows about the boys who went missing. If all of Wyatt's newspapers say nothing on the subject, I doubt Niven could have much knowledge of it either.

An older lady with a cane wobbles toward me as I'm gathering holds and placing them on the cart. She asks where she can find mature books.

"Large print?" I ask, about to point behind her, and tell her it's two rows over.

"No sweetie, the adult books," She whispers.

"We're in adult fiction now, what are you looking for?" I grab another book from the shelf, and slide it up against the last one in the row on my rolling metal bookcase.

She looks away and leans in, "I'm talking about the naughty books, girl." She stamps her cane, frustrated instead of embarrassed like I would imagine she'd be. I'm the only one left flushing candy apple red. I touch my warm cheek, and cover my mouth to suppress the giggles. Randy old lady.

I whisper, "They are mixed in with all the other fiction books. If you go to the front desk Janet will be able to help you narrow down some choices." I smile, hoping that a smile and my redirection will be good enough for her. I have no idea which ones would be considered naughty, and I'm not really interested in finding out.

As she walks away I wonder if I should give her that copy of Amish Wives Behaving Badly.

The cart fills quickly, and too soon I find myself standing by the front desk with an annoyed looking red head woman staring me down. Her nose is small, but so are the rest of her features, making her look cute even through her anger. She picks up three books, and fans them so I can see the covers. They all showcase a man's glistening, muscle packed torso. She blows into the air, fluttering her blunt bangs across her forehead. I smash my lips into a thin line as I hold in my laughter. It rumbles through my chest like an avalanche, getting louder and louder, until I need the counter to support me. I'm almost surprised I don't snort.

"What's so funny?" Wyatt comes up behind me, and I hear Janet dump the books into the return bin below the counter as she passes.

"Nothing," I say.

"Okay, whatever." He grabs a stack of thin paperbacks from a low shelf, and nods at me to follow him. I hear Janet, and the older man that helps out twice a week, shutting down computers as we shuffle down the hallway in the harsh light.

He spins around, half circle, to face me with wide eyes and tense arms. "You ready for this?"

"It's probably not going to work."

"I know, but it's worth a shot."

He hands me the book on hypnosis for memory retrieval, and I look at it shaking my head. "I can't believe something this specific exists."

He shakes his head as he takes a seat across the table from where I pull out a chair. I open to the post-it marked page, and start reading the monotone monologue.

"Come on." He has his eyes closed, and his mouth is pulled up to one side. "Say it like they do on T.V. and stop imitating Marge Simpson."

"I'm offended." I hold my head higher, tilting my nose into the air, and speaking in the best British accent I can manage. "This is how my voice naturally sounds whilst reading fallacious codswollop."

With his eyes still closed, he sighs. "I change my mind. Read it however you like, as long as it's not with that horrible accent."

"Just shut up."

The reading becomes easier when I finally stop thinking about how ridiculous it is. Being told you have to relax a thousand times, to me, doesn't seem like the best way to actually relax. By the time I read the last word I realize the font is a dark blue instead of black, and I'm annoyed by that for no reason. It's consuming my thoughts when I hear Wyatt mumbling under his breathe about something I can't understand. His head is limp, his chin sagging toward his chest, and his shoulders have fallen so far forward I'm afraid he's going to slip and hit the table with his face.

I'm leaning so far in that I'm practically crawling across the table, trying to decipher the words that barely make it past the tip of his tongue. "Eyes in the night." air rushes over the roof of his mouth when he breathes making a miniature vacuum noise in the silence. "Bone and flesh, my might."

It's some kind of weird poem. Where did he hear it? What does it have to do with his brother?

A black spot materializes on the floor in the corner of my eye, but when I glance toward it, it's like there was nothing there at all. Wyatt's hand slams down, hard, on top of mine. "Got ya!"

I'm sprawled across the table, and when he yells I slip forward and roll onto the floor, my heart beating war drums inside my ears.

"I will get you back." I say between breaths, with all inferred honesty in my eyes, since my voice is hushed inside my throat.

"Will jerky make it up to you?" he asks, as his digs into his pocket and tosses a baggy of dried beef at me.

I smile and take a piece out. "You're on probation."

"I'm heading back to the Kodak, this was a bust."

"I'm not going to say I told you so."

"Good."

"Because that would be redundant now."

He kicks my feet as he leaves, spinning me on the slippery floor. I get up and brush the dirt off my mangled jeans—my dad calls the holes ventilation. The first book I found Wyatt with this morning is on the top of the stack, and it's too easy, just lying there. I walk to the door and check the hall for Wyatt, since everyone else went home fifteen minutes ago. I close it silently. There's a dingy cloth couch on the far wall, and I make myself comfortable by propping up my head with a pillow. I kick off my shoes. I don't know what to expect, but I imagine I'd like to be cozy if I put myself into a trance.

Instead of treating myself to a monologue, I'm told to close my eyes and imagine my hallucination, manipulating them to my liking. The book says it's similar to being able to control your own dreams. I can't stop the smiles twitching at my mouth, the whole idea of hypnosis is embarrassing. Though, when I think about the visions becoming stronger, or worse than the bathtub incident, I can't think of a better way to spend my time.

"Here it goes."

CHAPTER ELEVEN

THE RISE AND fall of my chest is more hypnotic than the affirming phrases I'm supposed to be saying to myself. I will see things for what they are, if said one more time, might make me see this book for what it is: Total crap.

In spite of my feelings about the author, and his lack of skull contents, I continue my inner chant and focus my mind on the expansion of my lungs. It's at least twenty minutes in when I start to feel a little sleepy. Which isn't surprising. It's like a switch—it snaps in an instant—and I'm asleep, flat on my back with my hands at my belly button. Just as soon as my brain was off, it's on again—the gears of my mind spinning away. I open my eyes, but something doesn't feel right.

I can't move my head. Or my hands. I can't move at all.

The paralyzing dream-like state is completely disorienting. I can move my eyes, and from where I lay I see most of the room, but my breathing is even without my intervention. My body feels detached from my consciousness; I'm an alien inside a human host. I watch the door wishing Wyatt would come back from his research, but the likelihood of that is slim. He's scanning old newspapers for mentions of a haunted church, or his missing brother, and it's hard to get his attention even when he's in the room with you. He'll be there, while I slowly slip into insanity in the break room.

The door creaks, and my eyes snap to it, envisioning Wyatt's Converse high-tops entering the room before he materializes from the dark hall. But the door just languidly eases wider, showing me the blackness that can creep in on me while I lay paralyzed and unprotected.

Shadows slither in from the doorway like snakes, multiplying at a rate I can't even comprehend, but my heart rate doesn't even waver. Conflicting signals from my body make it even harder to concentrate on the reality around me. I try my hypnosis mantra, but the black wisps continue filling the room, coating the floor in a writhing haze.

A tickle pricks at my foot, feeling something like having my body dehydrated—slow, hysteria inducing torture. I will my body to move, to just let me relieve the itch that's slowly inching up my ankle onto my shin. My eyes strain as I peer down toward my bare feet at the other end of the couch. If my heart wasn't inhumanly steady, it would spike right out of my chest at the sight of at least a dozen spiders creeping up the length of my body. Inside my head, the pressure doubles; it thumps painful with blood, flushing my cheeks with warmth.

Their spindly legs stretch out below them, making their tiny bodies seem to float mid-air, and yet they weigh hundreds of pounds, pressing down onto me—suffocating me.

I sit up suddenly, covered in a thin layer of sweat, and completely out of breath. I wonder if it was a dream. Something shifts on the floor, but when I look toward it the tiles seem the same as always, a fluid blend of blacks and blues. My feet are heavier than normal, a blend of sleep and trauma, when I swing them from the couch to the floor. Something wet and skeletal smashes beneath my foot, and when I lift it the stringy guts and broken legs stretch between the tile and my heel. A spider. My mouth turns salty and dry with a strong urge to vomit all over the spider parts. I really hate bugs.

After scraping the arachnid's insides from my sole, I slip my feet back into my worn high-tops and search for Wyatt's Kodak. He's been there for over an hour, or at least, I assume, he's been there the whole time I was out. The maze effect of the shelves hasn't diminished at all, so finding him and his giant picture box turns into that scene from *This is Spinal Tap* where they're lost backstage. I swear I'm circling back on the carpet I just walked on when I see a light flickering around the corner, back toward the DVDs.

"Hey." I flip a chair around, and sit beside him at the huge glowing monitor. It's one of those ancient things that needs lifted with a crane, and its powerful light casts a blue hue on Wyatt's caramel skin.

"This isn't working. None of it." He lets his head slip

backwards on his neck. The way he lets it flop is sick and un-natural. I see his head snap off, and roll across the floor before I bring myself back to real life.

"You're just straight searching old newspapers front to back?"

"No, just the ones since the day he went missing and for six months after."

"Wyatt…" I sigh.

"I can't let it go, don't ask me to."

"I wasn't going to." I'm totally over trying to do that. "So do you have a feeling about if he's alive or not?" I choose the more optimistic word. He doesn't respond well when I tell him his brother is more than likely dead.

"I feel like he was attacked, or something, in that church."

"But we don't even know if you were really following…" I stop short when he gives me an irritated sideways glance.

"Just…" My thoughts are everywhere, trying to help him release his hold on this plan. "Can we come up with a better way to search?"

"I've tried every term I can think of in my Google search." His body slumps forward, and he smacks his head on the tiny sliver of table between the edge and the machine—which keeps clicking and humming waiting for its next task.

"Well then let's find anyone who used to work there, or whatever they call it, and track them down. Get a list of names as far back as we can."

He sniffs in a breath, quickly, through his nose. "I guess

it'll keep us busy."

"Hey wait." He sits up. "Didn't you say your sister used to do séances?"

I cringe at any mention of my sister lately. "Yeah, why?"

"She could contact my brother."

I shake my head. "Can we please not involve Mabel?"

"Come on, it could work."

"You really believe that?"

"Please?"

I shrug and nod. It's hard to say no to him.

I promised Wyatt I would talk to my sister, but said it might be a while before out paths cross again. I left out the part about me spending most of my nights at St. Dymphna.

I leave the library early with a plastic bag of vending machine food and The Shining. I saw the hardback fall through the return slot while I was stacking books to check them in. At first I laughed, thinking it would be a joke, but then I considered how bored Niven must be alone with just papers, and enough time to create life-sized models of the moon.

The air isn't as humid as usual, and I'm in a good mood, in spite of my strange evening spent in a partial coma, as I walk the stretch of wooded road that takes me to a now very familiar church. Dips in the pavement and loose rock are hard to see in the pitch black, though the outline of the church is perfectly clear with the streetlight illuminating it from behind.

The window is easier to open this time, and I'm upstairs

in an instant, taking the stairs by twos. The amazing moon is staring down at me, but the shining light of life I came to see is nowhere to be found.

"Niven?" I let my voice carry, but not too far, who knows what's lurking in the shadows here. No one answers, and I suspect he's getting food, or whatever it is he does when he leaves. I wish I could bring him home with me, but my dad wouldn't take too well to that idea. He barely tolerates me and Mabel being there.

"Hello?" I call again, but still there's only the faint chirp of cicadas in the woods. The bag in my hand suddenly feels heavier, reminding me of what I had brought for him. I place the book on top of his sketchpad, and the four bags of chips and two water bottles beside that. They haven't cut me a check just yet, but I was able to pocket some cash out of Dad's jacket. He can't remember if he spent it on beer or not, so it rarely comes back to me. I've managed to watch his drunken pattern closely enough to not cause any concern.

"If you're trying to scare me, it's working!" I yell out a little louder just in case. The silence is frightening. I've never been in the church completely alone, even if the first time I was here I thought I was alone.

"You're missing out," I say, softly, almost to myself, before I head down the stairs with my empty plastic bag. Something creaks when I hit the bottom step, and it sounds like it came from all the way across the room. The door behind the lectern, beside that giant sculpture, seems to sway when I look up, but in the darkness it's impossible to tell. Nothing but stillness is with me in the room, I tell myself. If it was something, it was just in my head. I know that to be almost ninety-nine percent true. There's always a one percent chance a creepy bone eating monster can use door knobs.

I take off running, and leap out of the window, the dry grass crunching beneath my feet as I land. The road makes me claustrophobic and paranoid—eyes appear in the bushes as I fly past. Something shuffles in the bushes ahead, and I stop my sprint to wait. I'm only about a half of a mile from home when a German Shepherd walks out from behind the vegetation to stare me down. I've never been around animals, and from what I know this particular kind is known for violence. I consider the statistics on it being just my imagination, but the memory of this dog as a puppy pops into my mind when I recognize the house he's coming from. What's his name?

He stops, mid stride, and waits for me to make the next move. When I shift a few steps to the side he mirrors my movements, and my stomach drops out of my body. It evaporates all the warmth in my body, leaving me as cold and still as a corpse. I don't know how dogs work, but I've heard to play dead with bears. Not like that sounds remotely like a good idea, and in all honesty, I'd most definitely run from a bear if ever the situation arose. No matter what I think, I feel strongly about sitting down in the middle of the road, and putting my hands out, palms upturned. So that's what I do.

He tilts his head, and walks over toward me. My heart

slows, and it's hard to breathe; I didn't know I was scared of dogs until now.

I feel like Buddha. My arms relax, and I sit cross legged with as serene of a look as I can manage, hoping I don't scare the dog. I take a deep breath as he sniffs at my fingertips. I try not to let myself think about how easily the animal in front of me could take one of my digits as a snack, if he wanted.

She! She. Her name is Bunny, and I remember the little boy who lives here rolling around the lawn with her sometimes.

"Bunny?" I whisper as she sniffs at my pants pocket, digging into it with her nose. The jerky Wyatt gave me pushes into my leg, and I quickly retrieve it to give to Bunny. She's very grateful. I'm just thankful to still be here on earth, instead of somewhere inside my head, for once. I get up slowly and back away—hoping she doesn't follow—but she's right by my side looking for more snacks. I've given her everything, but she's still sniffing at my pants like I'm holding out on her. She sticks her nose right into my pocket, and when I try to dig it out something comes with it: a giant spider. I screech, and jump away in horror, staring at the dead thing on the ground. Bunny grabs it by a leg and takes off running. I don't remember picking it up much less putting it in storage anywhere on my person. It was real? Where did it come from?

I pat myself down, searching for things that don't belong, but I'm left standing in the middle of the road empty handed. There's something both terrifying and comforting in that discovery. I consider the possibility that it was another one of

Wyatt's jokes, that it wasn't enough just to scare a decade of my life out of me, but he also had to put a dead spider in the plastic bag of jerky.

By the time I make it home, my jaw hurts from clenching my teeth. The house is quiet, but I sneak in anyway, out of habit. The darkness that never bothered me before is making my skin prickle, and once I make it to my bed I hide under my quilt and pray for morning.

CHAPTER TWELVE

WHEN I WAKE I'm still covered by the blanket; it's stuck to my face from sweating in my sleep, and I throw it off in a hurry to breathe again.

"When do you think your sister's gonna be home?"

"Wyatt!" I scream his name in shock that quickly turns to anger. "Will you please stop doing that to me?"

"But it's so funny. You scare with your entire body. It's like you're getting zapped by bug light."

He smiles even when I scowl at him. "It's not funny."

"Like a cartoon character. ZAP!" He throws his arms out in front of himself, letting his hair flop into his face, as he pretends to be electrocuted.

I try not to let it get to me, he doesn't know all the terrible things that are happening in my life. Things that are causing my permanently nervous state of being. I rub at my eyes, hoping to wipe away the pain forming in my forehead. "She leaves notes sometimes."

I kick some clothes around the floor, looking for papers. She usually leaves me something cryptic, just in case I really need to find her—she's strange like that.   With a hopeful expression, Wyatt holds up a post-it.

It isn't near, but not too far. If you want to, go ahead and bring the car.

"She's at Lucky Gun's." I grab the note and crumple it before throwing it into the trash bin.

"The bar?" he asks. I assume he's never been there.

"Yeah, about seven miles. A good two-hour walk." I sigh.

"Lucky for you, I have a car."

It's only ten minutes before we're sitting outside of Lucky Gun's, the most attractive thing Hannigan has to offer tourists. Shaped like an a-frame log cabin, and nestled beside a similarly styled motel, it's for those who want to sleep off the buzz, instead of dying in a fiery car accident on the highway. It's a Monday at lunch time, and the place is packed. People fill the patio watching sports highlights, and waitresses mingle around elegantly between tables. I've never actually been inside before.

"Let's go." His voice breaks into my dazed mind, and I have to blink a few times to refocus on the dashboard in front of me. His car doors are old and heavy, and mine swings back at me when I push it open the first time, but I'm ready for it the next time I try. We enter through the funky log doors, and squeeze through dense hordes of drunken men, who all seem at least a foot taller than the both of us. Don't they go back to a job after lunch, or does their height give them the correct alcohol to mass ratio for it to wear off fast enough? I grab Wyatt's hand to keep from losing him in the crowd.

We spot Mabel at the bar, bent over and kicking her feet in the air, giggling, and I'm surprised she isn't wearing a skirt to go along with the act. She always has an infectious spirit, and innocent manner, that unsuspecting men have no ability to fight off. She knows sports, cars, books, you name it, she can bull shit about it. She'll get right into your lap, and you'll never guess she stole your car keys.

"Mabel!" I shout from behind her. Her whole body slumps on the bar as she rolls over and leans against it to glare at us. She spots Wyatt, and her glare turns sticky sweet.

"Who's the cutie?" She tilts her head in her signature way.

"You already met him, and he's broke," I yell.

She rolls her eyes, and grabs his face in her hand, smashing his cheeks together making his lips pout. "He's still cute."

"I need your help," he says through fish lips.

"Oh, do you?" She smiles, and her eyes narrow. I can't take her act a second longer. I grab her bangle covered wrist, making her drop Wyatt, and drag her outside to his car. The mid ninety's cutlass is hot to the touch from the sunny day, so I opt not to lean against it.

"We need you to contact his brother," I say.

"God, Brenna." She pulls a cigarette out of her back pocket, it's smashed but she still manages to light it. She drops the lighter into the pink purse that never leaves her shoulder.

"What?" Wyatt looks worried. I don't blame him, I'm worried too.

"I can't believe you think any of that crap was real." She takes a long drag on the pathetic little stick.

"You said—" I start, but she interrupts.

"I said whatever I wanted. I liked to freak you out, baby Brenna. You spaz out like when you scare a cat and it flies into the air."

Wyatt laughs, "She totally does!"

I'm ready to punch her, right in the throat, but Wyatt steps between us. "I swear I'm repressing something. I have these dreams about something in the church on 12th street eating my brother. He's been missing for eight years."

"He probably just got out of this hell hole." She drops the cigarette on the broken pavement, and pivots the tip of her black flats into the burning ash.

I feel the need to help his case. "I saw it."

They both look at me. Wyatt, a slightly hurt curiosity, and Mabel, an unconvinced annoyance. I shrug.

"Fine. Whatever." She adjusts the bag on her shoulder. "Get some candles and I'll meet you at your house. It's the one beside Greg Wakes', right?" He nods.

She marches back into the bar, and I wonder how long we'll wait for her tonight. She's anything but punctual.

To say that Wyatt's mother is a soulless walking corpse would be a massive understatement. I haven't experienced the kind of grief she has, but I can't imagine turning into something worse than death. She stands in the doorway to the kitchen when we walk into the hallway from the garage, her short black hair is plastered to her cheeks and forehead, reminding me of a wrinkled Joan Jett in a rain storm.

"Home from work, or on your way out?" he asks as she passes us, brushing against me without a word.

"Going to bed," She mumbles. Her bedroom door closes with a heartbreaking thud. I'm afraid to say anything, even to ask what she does for a living.

"Sorry about that." He scratches his head with the hand not holding the bag of cheap candles. I shake my head with a shrug. He drops the bag onto the counter, and starts digging in the fridge.

"Do you like scrambled eggs? It's all I really know how to make," he says as he pulls an egg carton, and a half gallon of milk, from the fridge. I smile and nod, wishing he had something to throw in them other than milk.

"Can I help?"

After I suggest some add-ins for the food, we clean a spot at his kitchen table to sit, and as I move a pile of old mail onto the chair beside me, I can't help noticing a name on the envelope: Dennis Kline. I wonder if that's his dad, and if he has the same grief stricken existence as his wife. I don't ask.

"This is really good." His mouth is full of spruced up breakfast food, and he finally looks less unhappy. Not one of the sarcastic smiles I see frequently, but a real light in his eyes. I'm afraid it's because of what's happening tonight, and absently rub at my temple to calm my growing anxiety. He's getting his hopes up, and it's making me sick knowing how unlikely it is that we'd actually contact his brother's spirit.

"Yeah, well, there are only so many days in a row you can take plain scrambled eggs before you end up drinking your dad's beer for variety."

He chews slower as he looks at me.

I grimace. "Stop looking at me."

"My parents aren't ever home. They wouldn't notice if you crashed here."

"Dad wouldn't make it to work, ever. One of us has to be home." It's true, he'd never go into work. He'd just sleep late and blow it off. I'm not positive he actually gets to the factory, but the checks still end up in the mailbox every week.

"Ok. Well the garage number is my birthday, just in case."

I stick my tongue out at him when, with a smirk, I remember we have the same birthday.

"So," He starts, chewing on his thoughts, "what were you up to before you were chased into the library?"

"Surviving," I laugh. He doesn't.

I swallow. "I don't really have friends to hang out with."

"Well, you have me."

"Now," I retort.

He looks angry. I can't help my mouth sometimes. I

push my eggs around my plate as I clench my jaw; this time screwing up my friendship is all my fault.

"I'm sorry."

"I don't really have friends either, if you haven't noticed," he snaps, and pushes his chair back from the table as he takes his plate to the sink. He drops it in, more carelessly than I think he would normally.

"Wyatt, I'm sorry." I can't think of anything stronger to say. "I'm just careful about people, I don't have much luck with honesty."

He runs some water over his plate. "I'm the opposite."

He's gazing out the window into his wooded backyard, looking as abandoned as I feel. It's suddenly frustrating to know all the people around me are so self-absorbed. Though, I don't know his dad's story, he seems to have the same problem as me: selfish family members.

"What do you mean?" I ask.

"I assume people give a shit about how I'm feeling, whereas you don't believe anyone could ever give a shit about you," he says it like someone does actually give a shit about me. I know that to be untrue.

I shrug, and change the subject. "So we need some of your brother's things to do this tonight. Can we go on a scavenger hunt…" I wait. "Or would that be too hard?"

He looks at me. His blank stare is haunting, making my already wobbly chair even more uncomfortable. Finally, he motions to follow him to the basement.

Wyatt's basement floor is cold. I kneel at the bottom of a metal shelf full of white legal boxes, searching for anything about his brother. There's nothing but old business documents and receipts, dumped inside haphazardly, and covered in dust from the holes in the lids. I get up, and find my way through the clutter of children's toys, and unused gym equipment, nearly tripping over a lone pvc pipe sticking out from the mess.

"Find anything?" he asks from across the expansive grey room.

I shake my head as I come up closer to him, tip toeing over a broken tiffany lamp, and some plastic crates.

"Sorry for the mess." He blushes.

"I doubt all this is yours," I say, and he nods.

"All I really have is this photo." He'd brought it down from his room while I was going through a laundry basket of old polaroids.

"If it works," I say, then regret it. I should be giving him hope, to keep him from slipping back down into that hole he's dug to bury himself in guilt, but I'm naturally inclined to be a realist. Though lately, my imagination tends to forget that about me.

"If it works," he repeats.

We stare at the photo of eight year old Wyatt with his blonde brother. They look nothing alike, aside from the nose that Wyatt seems to have grown into since his elementary days. Where Wyatt is broad, his brother is narrow—shoulders, hips, forehead. His brother's smile lights up his entire face, and it's contagious. A desire to see Wyatt smile like that surges through me, but my enthusiasm falls to the pit of my stomach when I glance at him. He's holding back tears that would likely stream past his trembling lips, if I wasn't sitting here.

"It'll work," I whisper, then put an arm over his shoulder.

Mabel shows up at nearly midnight, but I hadn't expected anything different. We set up in the corner of the basement, where me and Wyatt had wasted the afternoon watching old cowboy movies on a tiny TV, admitting that we wished we'd lived back then, digging for gold or farming all day.

"No," Mabel scolds, "like this." She lines each candle up beside the other until from above, it looks like a pentagram. Well, like a pentagram minus the circle encompassing it.

"Isn't that the symbol of the devil or something?" Wyatt squeaks.

"Sit at the top point." She instructs with confidence, ignoring his comment. I'd never paid much attention to what she shaped the candles like, or what she said during these things, so it made as much sense to me now as it ever had. Which is very little.

He shifts a little to sit at the top point of the star, and Mabel pushes me to a bottom point, then she takes a seat at the other. We start the tedious act of lighting every candle with BIC lighters, and by the end my thumb is numb and permanently bent ninety degrees.

"Nobody breathe," I joke. Wyatt gives me a nervous glance, and I smile like I'm not freaking out. Even though I am.

"Give me the photo." Mabel has been ignoring me since she got here, and I don't know what her problem is, but I'm grateful I don't have to do much with all this garbage.

"Close your eyes. Then think about your brother, and only about your brother. We're going to try to speak to him through you." I start to wonder what her deal was at the bar earlier, she sounds so sure of herself as she speaks.

She takes my hand, and motions for me to take his. We're linked, making the circle for the star. She closes her eyes and Wyatt does the same. I catch her eyes when she opens them again, a split second later, and suddenly she winks at me before closing them again. Silence is all I hear for a few minutes before the floorboards above us creak with a ghostly moan. I'm afraid his mom woke up, and the scene plays across my eyelids. She lumps into the basement, and her placid manner changes to a motherly rage. She roars to life, knocking over candles on her way to strangle the girls who are corrupting her sweet son. A basket of blankets catch on fire, and we're all scrambling to get out of the basement, which quickly fills with smoke.

A choking noise from the circle snaps me out of my fearful vision, and my eyes search the room. I look Mabel up and down, but she's still and breathing evenly. Wyatt gags beside me. I try to separate our hands, but they're glued, palm to palm, to the other two in the room. Drool falls from the corner of his mouth as his throat refuses to open for air, and there isn't anything I can do but watch, panic stabbing at my ribcage, threating to show me how he feels.

"Stop it!" I scream at no one, because my voice doesn't work. I'm being forced to helplessly witness my friend's impending death.

Suddenly, he stops. His head slumps, and I see he's breathing, although it looks shallow and probably isn't doing much for his consciousness.

"Brenna." There's a new voice in the room, airy but full of life at the same time. I search my surroundings and find a transparent form materialize beside Wyatt.

"Don't let him blame himself," the skinny figure says. "He couldn't have done anything to help us."

Three more boys form in the room, far behind the first.

"You're his brother," I say. Finally my voice works.

Mabel's eyes open, and she's staring at me. I look from her back to the boys.

"I'm Lewis," he says, and introduces the other boys as his friends who died that day with him.

"What happened?" I ask, as Mabel frantically looks around the room for who I'm talking to, our hands still firmly cemented together.

"The bone-eater," he says.

I shake my head; that's what Niven said it was. A soul devouring, bone crushing monster.

"Promise not to let him near that place, please." He looks down at his little brother's hunched body.

"I can't promise that. People don't listen to me."

"You have to keep him away from there, he needs to let me go."

I'm shaking, near convulsions, at the sight of this thing in front of me, but I'm able to keep my voice steady. "He needs closure."

Lewis's static-like body pulses, and his face falls to depressed anger. I'm hit with a hurricane wind-like force, and slide across the floor, smacking the wall and curling into a ball of pain. My vision is blurred, but I see the candles swell before they extinguish, and I watch Wyatt's body hit the floor with a sickening, sweaty skin sound.

"Brenna!" Mabel rushes to Wyatt's side, pulling him to sit. He wheezes, taking in shaky breathes as she helps him upstairs.

I start crying. I can't help it.

CHAPTER THIRTEEN

IT TAKES A half hour before the uncontrollable shaking, and fountains of tears, subside. I venture upstairs, slightly disoriented and there's laughter from down the hall. I press myself to the door to better understand the muffled voices.

"You seriously pawned a guy's watch while he slept, replaced it with a cheap knock off before he woke up, and got him to buy you a new purse?" Wyatt sounds enthralled by my sister. She has to have some sort of boy beacon; they all fly toward the light too willingly be electrocuted. I'm hesitant to interrupt their conversation, to tell them what happened when they are obviously having a good time, and I'm not even sure how to explain it all. It's starting to feel like a dream, and with everything that's happened it most likely is to some extent. Just another of my delusions.

"Is it better now that I took a shower?" Mabel asks, sniffing her hair.

Wyatt drops his smiling gaze to the side. He notices my form in the shadows and runs to my side. "What happened?"

"Stop." Mabel takes me around the waist and away from him. "Take your time baby sister."

We all sit. The living room furniture is a worn brown leather sofa set and a glass coffee table that fits in well with the rest of the house, but it all feels sterile compared to the basement's cold and cluttered décor. Wyatt can't tear his gaze away, a nerve-wracking contrast to Mabel's overly comforting arm rub. I'm not that small; I don't understand why people have to cuddle me like a child.

"Your brother told me to keep you away from the church," I start.

He's trying to stay level-headed about it all, but I can see the emotions running across his face in quick succession: shock, anger, disbelief, and self-doubt. The feelings aren't lost on me, even after seeing it—and feeling it—I'm still hesitant to believe anything actually happened.

"How do I know—" he breathes, slowly. "Did he say anything else?"

"He introduced Tony, Jonah and Craig. I guess they died too."

His fist is invisible at the speed it flies through the air, coming down hard on the coffee table. He rakes his hands through his hair a few times before pulling on it harder than I think he should.

"Why?" he yells toward the floor. "How come you guys

got to see him?"

"Oh, babe, I didn't see nothing. I said that before," Mabel interjects, with a wave of her hand.

"Just you?" he asks me.

I shrug.

"Damn it," he sighs.

"Wait," I say, "So those boys were with him? That's how you knew it was real?"

He nods and I immediately stand. The urge to leave his house overwhelms me, and I start for the front door.

"Hey, where are you going?" Mabel asks.

"I don't know." Anywhere but here. Anywhere I'm not thinking about ghosts watching me from the corner of the room. Anywhere I can get my heart to stop racing. "Home."

"I'll drive you two home." He stands, but I put out my hand and make on the sternest face I can manage. He doesn't sit. "I can't let you guys walk all the way home in the middle of the night!"

"I do it all the time," I snap, "Since before you wanted me to help you Google monsters, or hypnotize you, or talk to your dead brother!"

His expression falls flat and his eyes widen in disbelief. "What?"

"Just stop pretending that you're looking out for me, it's pathetic." My feet on the wood floors are louder than I expect, but I can't contain the energy flowing through me. I wait for Mabel to follow, but she doesn't come. I open the door, but before it shuts I hear: "I'll help you clean up the basement."

She's already forgotten about me.

I pass under broken streetlights avoiding skateboard sized missing chunks of sidewalk—when I can—as I walk home, and everything pulls at my mind in every possible way. I can't pick one ridiculous thing to focus on. I saw something in the church, and now this ghost tells me the monster there killed him and his friends, so it has to be true, right? I've imagined a swat team invading a neighbor's house, swore that my hair turned to snakes, watched my sister drown in a bathtub of talons, and was nearly consumed by spiders and shadow snakes. How am I supposed to know what's real, and what's just an elaborate movie scene from my brain's constant reel? Wait until something kills me?

A chill runs up my spine, and I hug myself, wishing again that I had Niven's hoodie. The walk through the good part of town to mine isn't that bad, but it's too quiet, something that makes my thoughts even more unstable than they already are. A gut wrenching squeal echoes in the darkness. An unlatched gate swinging wild in the wind, banging against the metal locks that can contain it. I focus on my sparkly purple sneakers, and refuse to let it scare me. My shadow comes and goes with the downward cast of yellow light, feeling more and more like a black cloud following overhead.

I can keep it together.

Just focus.

A knot builds in my throat when I try to swallow, dry and

choking me until I force it down. The sharp, deep boom of a dog bark splits my chest in two, pouring fear out of my ribcage like blood out of a stab wound. I stumble on a rock, barely keeping myself upright and don't waste a second. I press my feet flat to the gravel as I run full speed until I'm out of breath right before I hit my street. Panting, and limping from a char-ley-horse in my calf, I stumble through the front yard toward my house. I need to stop letting my fear control me.

My room is how I left it; clothes kicked to the corner and bed sheets askew. Looking for notes is like second nature—a nasty habit—and I find myself flipping over bags and laundry baskets for a small yellow square. But I don't see any.

I sift through the clothes pile in the corner, looking for a familiar black hoodie, but can't find it anywhere. After a few seconds, I start to really flip out. Shirts and pants hover above me in a cyclone of cotton as I rage around the room. Violent-ly, I flip Mabel's mattress up, and lean it against the wall, sure she's hidden it, but come up empty handed. I can't go back to him without it.

Every article of clothing in the closet is part of the foun-tain I'm producing. On the bright side, it's ninety percent Mabel's stuff. I don't even care when I rip a white lacy thing as I'm searching—I'm too angry to care. How can she be so self-ish? How could she just take it? She had to have noticed it smelled like boy—an amazing, sweet smelling boy. I grab the lace shirt from beside me and rip it completely in half, savoring the lovely noise of ruining something of my sister's.

I look down at the two pieces, and the cork keeping my fury bottle up pops, draining me, down into the pile of Mabel's crap. My body melts with the fabrics and I gasp on a few tears before I pull it together again. It doesn't help. Not any of it. I wipe my eyes with a straw sock. It won't change her. I can't change her, or anyone else. I'm all I have.

One by one, I hang everything back up. After putting the bed down, and fixing her pile of shoes, I stare at the lace shirt on the floor and wonder if she'll notice its disappearance. She has so much, I can't imagine she has a mental inventory. But I'm worried anyway. I creep down the silent hall of my tiny sagging house, and out the back door to throw the scraps into the garbage bin.

CHAPTER FOURTEEN

As I STUFF my books into the tiny spaces between other books I zone out, worrying that Wyatt will hate me for what happened the other night. For avoiding him. I haven't had a conversation longer than two words with him in two days, which wouldn't have been weird two weeks ago, but now it's peeling layers off my heart. I can't tell if he's angry or giving me space to breathe.

My knees hurt from squatting so often, and I'm frustrated by the overfilled shelf of new releases. The last book is a six hundred page sci-fi and I wish it would just beam itself up so I wouldn't need to put it away. After looking at the other shelves to maybe make room for it by moving other novels, I realize the bookcase is just full. No area left for more fictional words, absolutely no space for more half-vampire queens.

"Just lay it on top." I hear a tiny voice from behind me, and turn to find a miniature adult standing with three books clutched to her chest. Her arms are twigs in comparison to her reading materials, but she doesn't seem bothered in the least by the weight.

"On top of the shelf?" I ask.

"There." She points to the top of the bookcase, and I struggle to grasp how her bony arm manages enough strength to hold the books solo. "Just lay it up there, everyone looks up there when they go by."

I scan the crowd—a few older ladies from the local retirement center are the only adults, and since the summer is coming to a temperature peak, the kids who don't have pools are finding refuge in the cool library. There are two boys in the back of the library who won't stop kicking each other as they manage their online game accounts.

"Where's you mom?" I ask. Her tiny frame suggests she's a preschooler, but her speech makes me think she isn't far off my own age. Her voice is filled with a regal quality.

"She's at work, so Tanner is in charge. He's watching videos of dirt bike races on the computer." She extends her arm out at its length toward a boy sitting apart from the punchy ones, he's silently cheering at the something on the humming monitor.

I'm curious. "What are you reading?"

Her face lights up, filled with an emotion I remember feeling as a child when someone took an interest in me. "This one is like the Little Mermaid, except she's the evil one." She shifts the top book to the bottom of her stack with precision.

"This one is about people having to leave the earth because it's going to explode." Her deep blue eyes flit from the books to my face as she gages my reaction. "And this one is about a girl pirate who recruits animals as her crew."

"Wow." I try not to patronize her, but she's so tiny and cute it's a difficult task. "Which will you read first?"

Her eyes widen and fall to the floor in thought. "I don't know, and I'm still looking too."

"I think the one about the Little Mermaid sounds good, if it matters."

Her smile spreads from ear to ear, and shows a row of tiny teeth abruptly stopped by a gap or larger yellow tooth. She must be older, considering she's lost some teeth. I try to re-member when I lost mine, but my childhood is mostly a blur I'd like to repress anyway.

"Can I see it?" I ask, and she over-joyfully obliges. I scan the text and can't imagine reading something like it before Jr. High, but that could be because Mabel never took me to the library. "How old are you?"

"Six!" It's the loudest she's been since I met her. I hand the book back to her with a smirk.

"Keep reading, there's never a shortage of places to go when you have a book." It feels cheesy on my lips, but I can't stop it, and she doesn't mind. She smiles, and sits down beside my cart, her black chin length hair swaying above her shoulders as she gets comfortable. I look around to see if her brother will come claim her, but he's still too engrossed in the videos to pay any attention.

"How's that book?" I ask after about an hour of her following me and my cart like a shadow.

"Aubriella is so mean to her sisters," She says with a sour face. "If I had a sister I wouldn't be mean to her. Brothers are always mean though, and Aubriella doesn't even have a brother. She's like a brother."

"Sisters aren't always nice," I say, but decide to not take it further. "Your brother is mean to you?"

"Yeah." She folds the corner of her book's page and closes it in her lap. "He likes to call me names and tell my mom I took the candy from her drawer, but I only do that sometimes."

I laugh, "Well, don't take candy from your mom then."

"But he takes my books and scribbles in them too, and my mom thinks I do it. He can't spell and I can. Ridiculous doesn't have an E." She's scowling at her lap, and pulling at her thumb at the unfair memory she's retelling, and I can relate to everything I see flashing across her face. The blame, the anger, the hatred, but also the guilt from those feelings.

"My sister likes to scare my friends away," I admit to her. "She tells them lies about me or tells them she'll do something bad. I never know about it until my friends stop talking to me. Which has always left me with my sister as my only friend." I consider saying, you get used to it, until I realize I haven't.

"She won't let you have any friends?" She's shocked, and her little peachy face shows it. "I have a friend, her name is

Grace."

"What's your name?"

"Reagan!" She gets loud again, like it's the most amazing thing she's been asked all day.

"I'm Brenna," I say.

"I'll be your friend!" She's so excited I can't help but giggle at her enthusiasm. Happiness is the best kind of contagion.

Someone calls my new little friend from across the library, and they sound like they're in a hurry. I assume it's her brother when he appears, torn sleeves and cutoff jeans, from behind a book shelf. "Get your stuff, I'm leaving."

"I wanted one more book." She stands and gathers her giant books in a hurry, frantic to comply.

"I don't give a crap, get your stuff or I'll leave you here without a bike chain. Mom would be so pissed." He stands with purpose, and a building adrenaline in his limbs, shaking them out a little when she doesn't immediately move to his side.

"But—"

"No!" He bursts out with his whole body, his face turning inside out with frustration. "I'm leaving now! Right now!"

She looks back at me for an instant, and I see tears welling in her eyes before she sprints off behind him; her brother crushes her spirit and it makes me want to crush him. With my fists. I'm surprised when I punch a row of books, and they transfer all of my energy to the books behind them, which then fly off the other side, spilling to the floor.

"What the hell?" It's Wyatt.

"Sorry," I apologize, then frantically try to explain the phenomenon—without admitting my angry outburst—when he appears in the hole on the other side. I remove the books I punched to peer through to shelf. I smile when he does. His face is in the shadow of the shelves, but I can see the humor in his expression.

"Trying to squeeze too many books into the same row?" His eyes glance around in amusement.

"No. I fit them in just fine. They decided to escape when I wasn't looking." I put my hands to the cold metal, and rest my chin against them.

"Damn those," he says, pulling back to look down, "guides to knitting baby beanies. Always trying to get away."

I swallow hard when he looks back at me and holds eye contact. The look on his face is reminiscent of the last time I saw him, and it hurts.

"I'm sorry you thought I was just using you. It's probably why I don't have any friends…" He says.

I reach through the book hole for the disheveled ones in the middle of the two shelves.

"This research is kind of cool anyway, and I think I found something… If you're interested." He looks down at the floor, at the books I blasted to the other side.

"Sure," I say. He nods and disappears from the window of books.

I walk around the corner of the shelf to put away the

mess, and bump right into him. He drops everything he was carrying, and it scatters all over the floor between us.

"I have to deliver these books," he says, then clears his throat. "Want to come with me?"

CHAPTER FIFTEEN

WYATT'S CAR IS old, not old enough to be considered vintage or classic, just old. The four door Oldsmobile is old enough to last through the end of the world, with only a creaky door to show for it. The giant door makes a heavy, finger severing sound as I pull it with me. I flop down onto the mixed material seat—leather trimmed cloth—and adjust myself to sit straighter as Wyatt grips the bus sized steering wheel with one hand, and turns the key with his other. The thing sounds like it coughs a handful of times before it finally roars to life, and stays at a moderate growl for the ride to the other side of town.

I occupy myself by comparing all the visible parts to the parts in my dad's truck, to avoid saying anything stupid out loud. Last time I was inside this car I was completely distracted by the prospect of seeing Mabel, now I have nothing but the 90's style interior to fill my thoughts. The door handle is a shiny metal strip instead of a chunky plastic square, and the dashboard is sharp and hard plastic where the truck is round and flowing. Wyatt's hands stay at ten and two for the entire trip.

"Where are we going?" I'm playing the phrase, talk to your dead brother, in a loop inside of my head as I ask him. I want to take back what I said, so bad. I had no illusions about his brother being alive, but he did. Now it's kind of confirmed that he's gone. I can't imagine how that feels, but I know it isn't pleasant.

"Taking some books to a homebound patron." He says it like it's rehearsed.

"A little old lady."

"Yeah." He smirks at me, and for a second I feel relieved, until his expression falls.

"What?" I ask, but he just shakes his head and plasters a fake smile on before he looks back at me.

Silence fills the car again, the warm summer sun making it thick and sticky between us, and I stare at the chipped paint on my toe nails. The sandals I have on left a slight line on my feet, from where they refused the dust and dirt of the earth access to my skin. I shift the straps from side to side investigating the color differences, instead of paying attention to the roads, and when I look up I'm freakishly disoriented.

"Where is this place?"

"Past the school." The road is unmarked and there's no shoulder, just jagged edges that mesh with dry, dusty fields of tall corn stalks, and intermittent heaps of forest. Every couple of seconds the fields end in a patch of evergreens, then start right back up. Lines of green trees blur past my eyes as I focus on the dirty window, letting the scenery keep to the back of my mind. By the time we reach the driveway my eyes feel like pinwheels, going round and round.

The house is a cute brick rectangle, with a tiny square porch that juts out from the front wall. The porch is off to one side, with a side walk that used to be lined in flowers, but now it's lined with weeds, grass, and some dandelions; one daffodil is dying, limp on the ground, like an antelope in the middle of a lion heard. I pick the yellow flower to take to our home-bound patron, hoping it makes her feel less trapped—an emotion I'm feeling just thinking about her situation.

Wyatt rings the doorbell, and we wait for one single eternity before he glances over at me with a shrug. He tries the bell again.

"Do we just leave the books on the porch?"

"She told me there's a key in case she's asleep, or fell down." He flips up the mat, then looks under the nearby garden gnome. I reach above my head into a hanging plant and feel around, stopping at a small piece of cold metal.

"Found it." I say.

"Do you want a prize?"

"No." I squint at him, unable to gage if he's saying it in anger or fun. "I only require your swore loyalty to me from this day forward."

He laughs, and it's a good one that catches my heart in

my throat. "I will serve no other queen."

We're laughing and play fighting as we enter the house, and the first thing that hits me is the heat.

"It's not all that pleasant in here, is it?" He asks as he searches the walls, stopping at the thermostat to turn on the air conditioning. "Mrs. Morgan?"

"I guess you lose body fat as you get older?" I whisper in his direction as he peeks in the tiny dated kitchen. "So she's probably freezing all the time."

"I'm going out back, she likes the covered deck." He passes me, dodging some fake plants as he pushes a chair under the dining table.

"Do you stay to read her the books or something? Are you B-F-Fs?"

His shoulders sag, and his head slumps to one side, and I suddenly realize I'm pushing him again. Pushing him away because he's hurt me before, even though I know he's sorry. I shake my head, hopefully conveying my guilt, and head down the hall toward the bathroom. I imagine a lot of older people fall in the tub, or on the tile floor; maybe she's hurt and immobile.

The first door on my left is a bathroom, and when I look inside the shower curtain is closed. No light is creeping in from the window, and the mirror reflects the light I turned on in the hallway, giving the room a glow.

Suddenly, I hear the gurgles—the choking sounds my sister made nights before—and can't push my feet forward.

Yeah, she's fine now, but the memory of abandoning her cuts at my heart, so deep I expect to see blood pooling on my clinging t-shirt. There's a layer of sweat on my entire body as I step forward, one foot after the other, to check the tub for fallen elderly women. I swing the fabric to one side, and the metal hoops click together like pennies in a jar. Nothing.

Back out in the hallway I expect to find Wyatt coming for me, but he's not. I assume he's checking the property, more thoroughly than is probably necessary for the situation. Looking behind hedges, and inside of neighbors' garages. Sweat drips down my nose, tickling me so much that I start wiping my face with my shirt, it doesn't take long for the whole of my hand-me-down Danzig shirt to be drenched completely. At the next door I don't hesitate to twist the knob, and step right inside.

The smell hits me before the sight of the body—a mix of rotting meat and perfume. My feet step closer to investigate, disbelief propelling them forward, because it may be all in my head. Her brown, brittle looking body, sags in a rocking chair in the corner, and chunks of her white hair have fallen onto her shoulders. I get close enough to see something move, her eyes flitting to one side, but that's impossible. It's maggots. They pour from one of her eye sockets like a waterfall of naked bodies.

My stomach contents rumble on the verge of eruption, at the sight of a real, decomposing corpse. I run to the hallway, and I heave onto the carpet. I cling to the door frame, as everything my body has been storing for the last sixteen years empties out onto the blue loopy threads. Wyatt runs past my peripheral vision and a noise, not unlike the one I'm currently making, comes soon after he enters the room. I feel his hands on my waist, steady and purposeful, guide me into the living room as I wipe my face with the sweat stained shirt stuck to my stomach.

"Here," he says as we walk out onto the front porch, "Sit here."

"Thanks." I sit, shaking and dizzy, and listen to him on his cell phone with a 911 dispatcher.

"No. Not really an emergency, she's definitely dead." I feel the churning in my middle, but can't imagine I have anything left to give up.

"Myself and another. Yes. We were delivering books. Sure. How long?"

He continues with his short sentences for a few more minutes before I feel his arm brush against mine.

"Are you alright?" He wipes away the hair that's sticking to my face.

I shake my head, letting my face fall into my hands. The image of Mrs. Morgan's dried corpse is branded inside my eyelids.

We sit, for a lot longer than we would have if she had been dying rather than dead, and by the time the Officer Millard gets around to asking me questions, I'm nearly useless. "Brenna, I just need to know if you saw anything that seemed out of the ordinary inside the house. Can you say anything?"

I swallow. "I checked the bathtub, and she wasn't there. Why didn't she have family checking on her?" I start rambling off the thoughts that have been swimming in my head for the past half hour. "Why didn't anyone call her? Why did she have to die right in front of the fucking door?" I kick the tire of ambulance, and press my head against the hot metal of the truck.

"If you can't tell me anything, I'll have to take you to the station. This is serious, Miss Bowman." He sounds formal, and it's weird to hear. I look up at his shadowed face—his hat hides his eyes—and blink hard, willing my mind to answer simply. The truth isn't difficult. Except when a small voice inside my head keeps reminding me that there were tiny bugs pouring out of her body.

My eyes widen at the thought, and Millard sighs. "Fine."

"No!" I wave my hands. "No, wait." I look at the ground. "We were here delivering books, I checked the bathroom, then I opened the door and got a face full of dead body, followed by rotting meat smell. Happy?"

"Nothing weird, or out of place?"

"No," I say for the millionth time. "Just the weird of walking in on a dead body, that's the weirdest thing I've seen all day."

He takes a few more notes, and gives me a soft pat on the back, trying to be reassuring.

I close my eyes and tilt my face to the sky, letting the sun warm my skin and maybe burn the first layer off while I'm at it. If at all possible, I would like to shed all layers from this day, the day I was hit in the face with corpse odor hard enough to make me ruin the carpet. The whole situation is simultaneously horrifying, and embarrassing. When I finally shuffle as far as Wyatt's car, I let my body slump down beside the back tire, sitting lifeless in the dusty driveway of a week deceased old lady.

"I'm sorry."

I look up at his long face. "It's not your fault."

"I know, but I'm still sorry you found her."

I grab his hand, and pull him to sit beside me.

"Can we never talk about this?" he asks, after a few minutes.

"I would love that." My head is heavy, and I want more than anything to rest it on his shoulder, but the fear of a possible negative reaction pulses through me enough to keep me upright. I feel a tickle on my cheek and realize he's let himself lean onto me.

It's a comfortable position—his head on my shoulder, my head against his—and we stay like that as we watch them carry Mrs. Morgan out on a stretcher, and tape off the property. The house seems sad and empty; she took its life with her when she left. I think of my dad, and how it would be if I left. Or if both Mabel and me left together. Who would call to make sure he wasn't housing fly larvae?

CHAPTER SIXTEEN

I WANT TO go home even less than usual after my encounter with Wyatt. I don't know how he was so calm after seeing a dead body, after smelling all that rank air that filled the house after I opened her bedroom door.

The mid-august air, normally hot and dry, is sticky and thick with the threat of a storm creeping on the horizon. A line cuts sharp across the atmosphere above me as dark clouds charge the puffy white ones, like a stampeding army. I'll be caught in the rain if I don't hurry home, but when I get to my street I find myself staring down the pot-hole littered road out to the church, and can't help wondering what he's doing. Alone when it's about to storm.

The Shining went over really well, so I make a habit of bringing a new book to Niven every night I can sneak away without being noticed. I bring him anything I hear Wyatt talk about, and a few I've read and never forgotten. The copy of

The Hitch Hiker's Guide to the Galaxy in my cargo pocket knocks against my leg as I jog through the narrowing street toward his hide-out.

The rain chases me through the front lawn, and I barely make it inside before the skies open up—they've decided that a giant waterfall should reside over our little town. I'm sure the cracked ground is thankful; the lawns have been desperately screaming of thirst for weeks. They'd recently started crunching a sad song of death when I walked on them to the library.

"Hey." I find him sitting upstairs playing a game of solitaire on the floor, and sit down next to him.

I shift the book to one hand, and lean in to finish a column out with 3-2-1. He bumps me with his shoulder, and draws three new cards from the deck. As he flips cards, and stacks others, I'm taken back to when I used to play cards alone in the tree house in the back yard. It was my own space until Dad caught Mabel kissing a boy in it, and, in a drunken rage, cut down the two trees it was built between. It crashed to the ground, into chunks of two by fours with nails protruding at odd angles—not unlike most of the church we sit in—taking my childhood innocence with it. Mabel had turned fourteen that month.

"What's spinning around in there?" he asks, peeking at me from the corner of his eye. Only one of his eyebrows is arched as he contemplates his next move, and when he flips over a card in an empty spot, a queen is revealed. She's sick and skinny, skin sagging from her bones, resembling Mrs. Morgan far too much for my liking. I feel nauseous again, like I might vomit all over his well-organized rows of cards, and I grab the Queen before my head starts spinning. "Where did you get this?"

"What?" His eyes expand like balloons, something I've only ever seen in cartoons, as I show him the card.

"This," I say, "What's up with this crap?"

He picks up the box from behind his back. "They're Halloween cards. Jacks are Zombies, Queens are Mummies, and Kings are Vampires."

He picks through the stacks, and shows me examples of the gruesome artwork that calls the stiff paper home. It's all legitimate, and neither in my mind, nor a horrible gag. I sigh loudly, and close my eyes. "I'm just so done with weird, I'm sorry."

I tell him about Mrs. Morgan, as well as the embarrassing bodily functions, and instead of laughing he just turns toward me, taking my hands in his. "Are you sure it was... real?"

I'd definitely had that thought at first too. "Ambulance came to get her and everything. It was real."

He doesn't let go of my hand as he pivots back to his game, wiggling his fingers between mine as he considers his next move. I pick the book up from my lap and drop it by his cardboard box of belongings, peeking at what he has to hold him over food-wise, and it's not too bad. Peanuts wouldn't be my first choice, but since he's stealing things I don't fault him for not getting cashews instead. The showers outside don't weaken at all. I startle as light flashes in the distance, and I wait for the clap of thunder but nothing comes.

"I've played this seventeen times today, and haven't won once."

I shift around a few cards until it's an easy win. I know he could have won this round, and probably lied about the other games he played, because he watches me as I finish out the stacks for him. I can feel his smile on me and it's good a feeling—being needed—better than it feels to be used. There's a monumental difference.

"Thanks." He takes the back of my hand to his mouth, to kiss it softly, and gathers the cards up one handed. It's intoxicating to be kissed by him—almost deadly, when his eyes peek out from his lashes. For a split second, I think he's gaging my reaction. The quick glance burns hot on my face, even after he's done looking my way. How can everything of mine burn so hot when his lips are barely warm?

"What book do I have today?" he asks as he shifts, and lays down in my lap, looking up at me with his grass green eyes.

"You make it sound like work."

"Reading is work. You have to hold a book..." He pretends to hold a book in the air above him, bumping my nose with the back of his hand.

"Then you have to not hit yourself in the face with it when your hands fall asleep." His hands fall to his face, slapping his palms to his cheeks loudly.

"And you have to keep your eyes open, and not sleep." The rest is muffled through his crazy face massage, apparently it's his method to staying awake.

"If you have to keep yourself from sleeping, you aren't doing it right." I gather up the courage to run my hands through his messy hair, and it feels glorious. Soft and tangle free— something I could only wish for in my own hair. He makes a noise I assume is approving.

"What do you do when you aren't here taking care of me?" he asks with his eyes closed, like he wants to imagine a life outside the church's walls. My hand is rhythmically combing, from his hairline to where his head meets my thigh, as I think.

"I work."

"What else?"

"Avoid my family."

"So, I'm a distraction?" He starts tickling my knee with his thumb.

I frown. "You're a prize."

"For what?"

"Enduring a life of selfish friends and relatives."

"What makes you different?" he asks, "And how am I not selfish? I make you visit me in a creepy church."

"You don't make me." I push his head off my lap, and he thumps to the floor. Shock flashes across his face.

I lie down beside him, and take his hand as we stare up at the handiwork of men who are long gone from this world, like

Mrs. Morgan. "I visit you because they all bring me down, with their habits and obsessions, but I'm happy here. Just us, no issues."

I purposely ignore his first question, hoping he's forgotten it, because I really don't know what makes me different. I'm obsessed with getting out of town and far away from them, and then I have this new issue of being a diagnosable crazy person. The main difference is I'm not using them to get myself out of town, I'm going to do that by myself.

"How bad have you ever gotten in trouble?" he asks, and my heart picks up its pace. I see my dad's face, indifferent, as he back hands me for refusing to give him the car keys after he's been drinking. I see Mabel, walking the halls in high school with a group of girls. Walking and laughing. They had pointed fingers, blaming me, for spray paint on some new girl's locker—paint with the word *whore*. I would never.

I try to form a thought to respond. "It depends," I say, "I get in trouble all the time for things other people do, or things that are I think are right. It's pretty ass backwards in my world."

"One time I shaved off my dad's mustache… he takes sleeping pills." He snorts out a single laugh, and smiles to the air.

"I've thought about cutting my dad's pony tail before, and I could because he's always passed out drunk," I say, "But I knew he'd take scissors to mine in return."

I clutch my hair with my free hand, and he shifts beside

me. He turns on his side and kisses my cheek. It's soft and breathy, and he lingers there for a long time, stirring my insides around in a hot mess of emotions. My face is warming, and my hands tremble at my sides—I've never felt so comfortable, yet so completely uncomfortable at the same time. The inability to form a full sentence in my head makes me nervous, and I sit up, letting go of Niven's hand.

"What?" His voice is close to my ear causing the surface of my skin to vibrate. I'm confused, and so disoriented I can barely breathe. I know I like him, I know how things work when you like someone, but the intensity is making me dizzy, and sick on emotions. It's too much, keeping everything bottled inside; not just the feelings I have for him, but everything I've felt for anyone. It's all falling down on me, weighing me down like a brick tied to my foot, and I'm drowning in it. He scoots closer—only making the pressure worse—and I press my hand lightly to his t-shirt. He lifts my chin toward him. We're a tangle of legs, twisted like licorice, but not nearly as sweet. I can feel him leaning in, even though I've had my eyes shut for a while. Something tells me to pull away, even though I want to kiss him. I think.

A bolt of lightning hits a tree outside, rattling the windows and shaking the room violently. It's close, by the road, so it doesn't take long for the rumble of thunder to follow. I take the break in tension to push us both back down on the floor, then I curl into his chest. His hand finds my hair and with every stroke he combs down my back, I feel less intoxicated.

Though, in its absence, a slow growing sense of dread fills the void.

CHAPTER SEVENTEEN

LATE NIGHT TURNS to early morning, which quickly turns into late for work. When the sun stretches its fingers through the topmost limbs of the trees I reluctantly get up from our comfortable body cocoon.

"Just skip it." He says.

"I can't." I slip my feet into my boots as I flatten my shirt the best I can. "I need the money if we want to leave here."

"I could just steal my dad's credit card." He offers as he stands. He takes my hand, and pulls me against him, flattening our bodies together, and I'm momentarily dazed.

"I…" My voice is breathy and soft, and I can't force more solidity into it if I try; his mouth hovering by my forehead is ruining my ability to focus for the rest of the day.

"I could steal his car too. He's too busy to notice anything half the time."

"But he would report it, we would get caught, and then

where would we be?"

He considers my reasoning, his mouth twitching slightly at the corner—the almost smirk, I've learned.

"Just let me make some money, enough to pay for gas across the country—"

He interrupts, and I pinch my lips together watching him talk. The movement his mouth makes is beautiful, but probably only because I want to bite it. "With what car? Where will you get a car? Just because you have money for gas—"

"I'll find something." I cut him off with confidence. I will find a car, I may even buy one.

"I have to go." I say, and he holds onto my hand as I move to leave. I turn to give him an annoyed look, but he's smiling. "Stop it."

His smile widens, and my face burns without my consent, the warmth spreading over my entire body.

"I have to go," I say again, and he nods.

I stop at the top of the stairs, and hold up the sci-fi book I'm taking back with me. "How did you like it?"

He shrugs, "It was alright."

"I thought it looked good… do they find a new planet?"

"Aren't you late for work?" He joins me at the stairs, and kisses the top of my head. "Go."

The all night rain left puddles in the pavement where there used to be holes. I narrowly miss soaking my feet in cold water a thousand times, and I decide to be more cautious. I hate the slosh of wet shoes. As I pass the clinic, jumping to miss another shimmering death trap, I hear a long creak in the distance. Hinges on the police station door make a metal screech that can be heard even through the relentless chattering of birds on the telephone wire above. But today it rings deafeningly loud inside my head, unhindered by ambient noise. I'm frozen in fear, anticipating the persons who may be exiting the building across the street. Will they be balding country boys? And if so, can they please be limping or in casts?

I watch the door from the shadow of a wide evergreen tree, and find myself retreating to the safety of its branches. Officer Millard steps out, and down the three concrete steps to the parking lot asphalt—two men in handcuffs follow close behind. He turns and unlocks their restraints, and my lips trace the word "no" over and over again on the air. Their truck isn't in the visible area, but I can only imagine it's in an impound lot somewhere if they were arrested. Nate has a neck brace, but other than that they seem too good for the beating I thought they received. The bone crushing, metal bat blows still ring in my memory, and make me nauseous.

I instinctively crouch into the tree-line as I watch them chat with the officer. It's too easy. They're nodding and acting like friends, but Millard saw them with me, he knew. Why is it so easy for him now? They said Mabel stole something, maybe they're all finding common ground in their hatred for my sister. We should form an anti-fan club.

They shake hands, and walk separate ways; Millard back

toward the police building, and the men toward the gas station. They're limping, only slightly, and I wish it was worse; their good health makes me angry. As they walk into the tiny convenient store, I venture out of the brush to leave. But as soon as I step foot on the road, I hear the hideous rattle of a tiny bell. A bell above a door. When I look toward the noise, all I see is Danny's sneer. My breath catches in my throat as I stare at his vengeful face. Then I take off running toward the church. I escaped them in there once, and this time they aren't as physically fit to run after me.

My feet pound the wet street under me, and it echoes through my legs sending shock waves of panic through my heart. The damp air sticks in my lungs, making it hard to breathe, and I'm gasping for oxygen by the time I crawl into the window. I kick it shut behind me, with everything I have.

"Niven!" I fall into the sanctuary, pain stabbing at my heart and lungs, and all I want is for him to tell me they didn't follow me. They weren't ever there. They never got out of jail. But when I see him bounding down the stairs, I know they're somewhere close.

"They're back." He comes up beside me, both of us staring at the door we know they'll come through.

"I'm dead."

"Not yet." He looks around purposefully, and I hope with every ounce of my soul that he's stashed a gun somewhere, because that's the only thing I can imagine would help us now. I lunge toward the stairs, and fall up them a few times before

Niven takes me by the elbow and helps me to the giant window. I have to see it—them—for myself, with my own eyes. He's taken the moon down, and if I had time I'd be devastated, but I just smash my face to the glass and pray they aren't out there looking to get inside. But they are. Slightly broken in body, but renewed in spirit; they want to skin me alive. I watch them as they pace the front lawn looking at all the doors and windows.

I feel his body beside mine, and start to shake my head uncontrollably. "I'm dead." I repeat it again, and again, until he puts a hand through my hair, brushing it out of my eyes and tucking it behind my ears.

"What if we get them lost? There are a few doorways, not much light... We could trap them somewhere."

I absently ignore him. "My dad had a bat. We need a bat."

"Brenna!" He shakes me, and my eyes snap to his. "We need to confuse them, and scare them."

"How?"

"It echoes really well from the balcony, I could pretend to be you from upstairs."

I shake my head. "They'll just follow you upstairs."

My stabilizing nerves don't have much time before they're thrown into overdrive again with the sound of the window crashing open. Sounds of floorboards grunting and creaking seep into the room from the crack under the door, and I'm breathing so fast I can't keep the black haze from creeping into my vision. I may pass out, and become a very easy target.

"Calm down." He grabs me by the elbows and his nose grazes mine, his breath is minty warmth on my lips and my breathing slows, but only a by a fraction. "Come on, we have to get them into the dark hallway."

He drags me back down the stairs, and when we reach the door to the other side of the church I'm twitchy and tense.

"I'm dead." I repeat it until I hear the door across the room opening, and I stare at it unable to move.

"Hide." His voice is a whisper, and I immediately duck behind a pew to wait for the inevitable.

It takes them more effort than it should to open the first door, which gives me a little thrill knowing they didn't escape my dad completely injury free. The floor is covered in debris, and it's sticking to my legs as I lay flat on the floor watching their shoes shuffle around in the early morning light. They're taking their time exploring the room and aren't getting anywhere near my hiding spot. I think back to the day I first found myself in this towering room, and come up with a diversion.

I slap the floor in sync with their footsteps, creating an echo, hoping to invoke their worst nightmares to crawl the walls around us. They stop and start, testing to see if the noise is their own making, and Danny turns to his friend. "She's in here."

Nate is skeptical. "How do you know that's her?"

"I see her stupid purple sneakers behind that bench," he

shouts.

I propel myself onto my feet, and immediately regret it. He hadn't seen me. They weren't even looking my direction when he said it. He just remembered the shoes I was wearing and flushed me out of hiding with amazing ease. I stand, staring at two men, whose heads are dwarfed in comparison to their shoulders, and listen to my heart beat deafeningly loud inside my ears. I hear his voice thrown across the room, Niven's raspy tone beside my cheek, "The basement."

Their footsteps limp toward me as I pull at the door to the dark hallway. I quickly slip inside before they make it to me. The narrow passageway still smells of rust and rotten wood, and I back away from the basement door, toward the exit behind the altar at the front of the sanctuary. I trip over something on the floor, and gather myself together as the men open the door. The light from the sanctuary pours inside the hallway, but leaves me in the shadows, slinking farther back into the darkness.

"Come out, come out, wherever you are." Nate thinks he's funny.

"I'm going to gut that bitch once I get my money." Danny remarks with a fist to his palm. So, Mabel stole money, that's nothing new.

"Where did she go?" Nate looks right in my direction, and for a split second I feel his eyes on me and swear I'm done for, but then they both snap their heads toward the basement.

Danny starts a slow swagger down the hall, confident he's

finally found me. "Oh no, I think we lost her." His confidence is as sad as it is funny.

Slowly, I lower myself to the floor to stabilize my shaking knees. My hands find the floor, but it's holding secrets. As I watch the men open the basement door, I feel along a protrusion on the floor. It's a skinny pipe, likely broken off from a leak, and feels crusty with corrosion. I grip it hard, instantly feeling safer. If anything, I can slow them down with a blow to the face from a copper pipe.

"Just come out Brenna, it really smells in here." Danny calls into the small basement room for me, and I subdue a laugh that bubbles in my chest at his idiocy.

"What's that sound?" Nate backs away from the basement door; with each step he shakes a little more.

"Shut up—" Danny's rage is cut short by a screech that envelopes the room.

The sound wipes my mind clean of all thoughts, a scream of delight from a creature—not human and not of anything I've heard on the earth—rings through the hall, and I'm knocked onto my butt by the vibrations in the air. The pipe sits securely in my lap like the harness of a roller coaster. I flinch on instinct from the screams that come from the two men, it's like nothing I've ever heard from fully grown adults, guttural and frightening. The boarded window rattles, then a plank comes flying off, and I see Nate beating on the glass trying to escape something that's attacking Danny—something I can't see. I shift backwards, toward the other door, as slowly and as quietly as possible.

Nate grunts and screams as he tries to throw himself through the now uncovered window, but it's useless. It's nailed shut, and he can't fit through the broken glass squares. I wonder why he's not going toward the door, but when I see a shape in the blackness, I feel the onset of hysteria. The crazed fear he must be feeling, only tenfold. He slips to the floor, pulling half a set of curtains with him, and crab crawls backwards away from the crunching and cracking in the distance. I make it to the door, but I'm too afraid to open it. I'm also too curious about the screams, and the loud sound of snapping wood.

Nate stops cold. He isn't even shaking anymore, just still white flesh. I wonder if he's died from fear.

That's when I see it.

The long, stretched face of a human, with the shoulders of a werewolf—bony, gray flesh flashes in the rays of sunlight streaming from the dusty window. The black haze finds its way into my vision as my heart pumps at light speed; I can't pass out in here, not with that thing in the room. Its arms are longer than most men are tall, and it crawls out from the basement toward Nate like a beached mermaid. Its tail whips around to corral him, making it easier to attack, and its razor teeth drip Danny's blood onto the floor. It's like watching a snake prepare to strike, only it has arms to hold its massive head in the air. Its jaw unhinges like the clown at the end of the putt-putt course, and descends upon him.

The heat of my hands warms the copper pipe, reminding me of my physical presence in this massacre. I stand silently at the door, begging the creature not to see me. It's busy containing Nate, as he flails against its sharp tail made of bone shards. Its soft, wet, pliable flesh is littered with white jagged spikes that stretch the skin, or oozing flesh—whatever the monster is made of.

My hand is on the knob when it inhales half of Nate's body. It stabs its teeth into his middle and his screams don't stop, they are only muffled inside its massive head. I can hear him choking on his own blood, inside of its head, and my arm goes limp at the brass handle. The monster's eyes catch mine, and in an instant I'm on the other side of door holding it shut with all my weight.

Sweat drips from my forehead into my eyes, and when I wipe it away I notice my arm glistening in the shadows. I walk to the podium and stand under the warmth of the light streaming in, lifting my arms toward a non-existent congregation. The pipe in my hand is covered in deep red blood that flows down my arms in murderous rivers.

What have I done?

Shadows in my peripheral vision overtake me in blackness, and I feel myself hit the floor before I go unconscious.

CHAPTER EIGHTEEN

MY EYES HATE me. They want to leave my body and never return. They're caked with sticky gunk when I wake, and I rub them until it hurts to open them. My vision is blurry and monochromatic in the stillness of the church, and as it clears more colors appear—brown pews, green speckled floors, mahogany doors, and the dull rust red of my skin. The moonlight isn't comforting tonight, and it only serves to show me what I've done; rubbing my nose in the unspeakable things I did that I can't remember doing. I didn't just kill two men, I saw a hideous man eating demon do it in front of my eyes. Didn't I?

I stand, leaving the bloody pipe on the floor, and run through the church and out into the cool night air. I've been unconscious for the entire day and the oxygen rush, plus the abundance of blood, makes me so dizzy I have to stop halfway, to vomit. I run, avoiding streetlights and open road, until I get home. The house feels judgmental—it knows what I've done and it's turned out all the lights to persuade me to leave, to run in another direction so I can't hurt anyone else. I did want those jerks dead. Not just because they threatened me, but because their smug faces needed a clean slate. I find a puddle in the yard and scrape the dried DNA from my palms so I can unlock the door, evidence free.

I go straight to the bathroom and shut the door, locking it and staring at the knob as I back toward the tub. I get inside, fully clothed, and turn the handle all the way to the opposite side. I'll burn away the evidence. All of it. Burn their memory from my body with scalding water. It rises up from my ankles, over my hips, and I squeeze my pants trying to wring out the stains but they just seep into the clean parts of my clothing. I strip to my underwear and drop the wet clothes on the floor beside the tub, they immediately soak the rug and spread black liquid out across the floor.

The bathwater is pink, my arms sticky with the men's blood, and as I scrub residue builds under my fingernails. The color isn't fading from my body and I'm losing my lucidity. If I can't get it out of my skin, I'll have to just peel off the layers until it's gone, just like an onion. It can't be that deep. The wrinkles in my wrist look like a good place to start ripping it away. Tears streak down my cheeks, tickling on their way down, and sticking in different places on my face. I'm so covered in filth, water isn't going to cut through it.

Imagining what happened to Danny and Nate makes me

gag to the point I dry heave over the side of the bathtub. It's not bad enough to have lured them into a church with a monster, but I had to lure them in and become the monster. The palms of my hands ache from hot soapy water, and the force I'm rubbing them together. They're bloodier than before I started. They can't be though, it just has to be the heat. I keep telling myself it's the heat when I hear the crunching of gravel in the backyard—the bathroom window never closes in the summer. I feel like a deer, still and alert.

The door knob rattles and I scrub more, and more, until I'm sobbing and scratching at the skin on my arms, terrified of being found covered in blood.

"Brenna?" It's Mabel. She unlocks the door, zips inside, and closes it silently behind her. She's trying not to wake Dad.

I don't say anything, only continue trying to peel the skin from my bones.

"What are you doing?"

Through sobs and shaking, I mutter, "Getting out all this blood."

"What blood?"

I look up at her, dazed and tired. I haven't seen her since she was where I sit, black pits for eyes and talons creeping from her cold, limp body. I glance at my hands, then the water, and find it all completely normal. No blood.

"I…" My mouth twitches when I try to speak and nothing comes out, no matter how much I want it to.

"Come on, little one." She pulls me out by my armpits

and wraps me in a towel, then dumps the wet clothes into the tub and guides me to our room in the dark. The hallucinations are out of control and I have to tell someone. Someone other than Niven needs to know what's going on in my head.

Niven.

Did I hurt him? Was that his blood?

I look at my hands again—the towel that's draped around my shoulders starts to slip, but Mabel readjusts it to stay put—and there isn't anything but blotches of red from trying to clean the nonexistent murder scene. She sits me down on my bed, and drags her mattress across the floor to combine it with mine. Her hair is frizzy, pulled back in a ponytail—which isn't a normal style for her. Her makeup is running but she's sober, and confident, as she flips off our light and gets into bed beside me.

"Where have you been?" She asks in a whisper after curling up next to me.

"The library, working." I lie.

"I didn't see you there."

"Well, I do take breaks." Our voices carry only as far as the other's ears, and it feels like we're one person, talking inside our own head.

"I wanted to get lunch with you, Wyatt said you never made it in."

I try to turn away from her but she grabs my hand and holds me steady. "If something's wrong, you need to tell me."

She's not my mother, and she can't play like it whenever

it suits her. I grunt and roll toward the wall, then mentally kick myself for being stubborn; she might know something about our family history, maybe she has visions too.

"I know what happened yesterday, with that old lady."

"That's not it." I admit, but she clings to the idea like a leech.

"It's a big deal Brenna," she says urgently in her hushed tone, "You found a real life rotting corpse, that can't be unseen."

I don't care about waking Dad, I yell it like she isn't right beside me and it feels good to let it out, "Don't you think I know that?"

"I'm just saying, it's okay to not be okay." Her voice is calm even though my body is shaking in anger.

"You have no idea," I say. Something keeps me from telling her the truth; something about the way she's always up and down, hot and cold. I just don't like giving her all my secrets. Any of my secrets.

"Why did Mom leave?" I ask after a few minutes of cicada silence. The window in our room is open and the noise brings down our bedroom walls, if I close my eyes.

"I wish I knew." I've never heard her sound so honest, but I've also never asked her about Mom.

"Did she die?" I was only five when I stopped seeing her come to my room to kiss me goodnight.

"I don't think so, but Dad never said anything after she was gone. She just vanished."

"No note?"

"Nothing. I think she took some of her things though, so I've always imagined she ran away from Dad and his lovely attitude." Her sarcasm is so obvious a child could detect it, and I don't blame her. He's not even close to the easiest person to get along with.

"She ran away from us and my craziness."

"You were just imaginative, baby Brenna." She snakes her arms around my waist and hugs me tight.

I bury my face in my hands. "I used to write, Mommy grave, all the time."

"I'm sure she knew you were trying to write, Mommy brave. God, I knew that and I was barely seven."

It doesn't make me feel any better. She could have had hallucinations, just like I do, and something so simple could have sent her packing. Maybe we're exactly alike. Ready to run, ready to leave it all behind.

"Go to sleep, you have work in the morning."

I'm already dozing when she says it, and as I let the dreams of my mother's face take me I wonder briefly how Mabel knows when I work.

I wake to a loud bang. A door slamming not once, but four times. As I turn my head toward my bedroom door—waiting for the intruders I'm too tired to fend off—I realize it's the glass storm door, it's catching the hurricane force winds that have been pounding against the walls of the house all night. I think about our window, but assume Mabel closed it after I passed out, because the room isn't blowing away. My pillow shifts, and Mabel moves from it to her own while still asleep.

I'm not asleep for long before sounds of shattering glass sends me into an upright and fully awake position, breathing hard and heart pounding with the power of all the winds from the past night. I wonder what time it is when I hear voices from the kitchen muffled through the bedroom door. I get up and throw on some clothes before creeping out the door into the hallway. The sun rises into the living room, giving all the dust illuminated beams to dance around. I wave my hand through it wishing I could feel the tiny particles hit my palm. I turn toward the kitchen, and the mess that's my family.

"Stop trying to make me, I'm hung over." I see my dad tear open the fridge, reaching for a beer. It's his second, according to the pile of glass on the floor that Mabel is trying to pick up. She eyes me from across the room, her expression shame and disappointment. Something I understand too well. And not just when it's his behavior.

My jaw tightens as I stomp toward the refrigerator, slamming it shut before he can find another bottle of liquid avoidance.

"Brat." He pushes me hard, but not as much as he would if he was drunk. Sometimes when he's drunk he'll shove me across the room with enough muscle to slam me into a wall.

"Get dressed," I say forcefully, stepping back toward the door before he can open it. Mabel takes his arm, pulling him toward the bedroom. His eyes are locked on mine as they back away. I breathe through my nose, trying not to let any emotions show on my face.

"Come on, please." She guides him, and he stares at me with disgust—I'm hideous to him.

Finally, he yanks his arm from her grasp and heads down the hallway. "Quit it, babe. I got this."

Mabel sighs and looks after him. She doesn't look at me when she says, "You get to work too."

When I finally make it to the building, I hide in the tiny closet where the drawer from outside drops all the returns.

"Hey." Wyatt comes up behind me as I sit crossed legged on the floor, stacking books from under the slide. They're scattered all over the tiles because someone stole the bin, for whatever reason, and hasn't returned it.

"Can't we just go buy another box for this thing?" Two books fly out from the wall, and narrowly miss my head.

"We could, but it would be more fun to take a road trip."

"It's too soon for more trips with you, Wyatt." I don't mean it to be as harsh as it comes out and silence quickly fills the room.

"Sorry." He plays with the door to the closet. It creaks, and scratches the floor in one spot.

"It's just," I start to explain, "I've had a rough day, and it's not even ten in the morning."

"We're not working tomorrow, would that give you enough time?" He says please under his breath, like a little kid, and I know it has something to do with his obsession. He's taking me somewhere that might have something to do with his brother's disappearance.

"Is this about Lewis?" I look over my shoulder when I ask and he immediately looks to his feet, avoiding my eyes.

I pick up an armful of books, and stand at the doorway with him. He looks shamed, like I think he's pathetic, and even if that's true I don't want him to think it. I like him enough to be honest, but not to the point of cruelty. My head wavers, like the thoughts shuffling around inside of it. "I'll meet you at your house?"

He blinks a few times, as if he's still processing my words. "Yes. My house."

CHAPTER NINETEEN

IT SEEMS LIKE I'm picking books up off the floor for the rest of day. The extra hot weather brings in children by the dozens, and they never put anything away. When I get home, I'm surprised that I don't find Dad's truck parked erratically in the yard. Immediately, goose bumps take over my arms. He isn't always home, but it's rare enough that being gone twice in a week makes me edgy. I try to shake my head, and blink away the gruesome images of car accidents that flash through my thoughts. Crushed cars, shattered glass, and severed limbs littering the street under a blinking traffic light. I sprint into the house and look around the kitchen for something to clear my mind, even if it's scrubbing the cabinets with my socks again.

It doesn't stop, no matter how much I focus on everything else. The handle of the fridge is sticky and warm, plastic deteriorating from years of use, but I don't stop to clean it. There is an entire case of beer bottles sitting front and center for me—the light above it glowing an invitation to erase my problems. He does it every day, so it shouldn't be such a big deal to pop the cap off and throw one back. Everybody does it. Just because my dad can't pace himself doesn't mean it would be a problem for me. I reach into the box.

The bottle is cold, and condensation forms after just a few seconds of being in the humid air inside the kitchen. It's like my hands are crying for me, telling me to find another way, any other way, to get out of my own head. I set the beer on the counter to find the opener, and after searching every drawer I finally find it inside the fridge beside the box. The flat metal fits perfectly against the cap, one flick of the wrist and I'll hear that familiar pressurized pop.

The phone rings and my hands fumble around, barely catching the bottle and opener before they hit the floor. I brush off the dampness of my hands then lift the pale yellow receiver.

"Hello?"

"Brenna." It's Frank. "You need to come get your dad."

I roll my eyes. "He can't drive?"

"If he could, do you think I would have taken his keys and called you?"

"I guess not." I sigh.

"I pushed him outside with his forty, it's his third by the way."

"Why'd you let him drink three?"

He smacks the counter, I hear it through the phone. "I

didn't! I found him drinking in the corner. I'm doing you a courtesy not calling the cops and having him dropped in the tank. You better fucking thank me when you get here."

I hang up, shaking from anger and the shock of Frank's unexpected language. He's usually so calm, I've never even heard him raise his voice before. I wonder if there was anything between my dad and him, from a long time ago that I've never heard about. Frank seems to have a sore spot when it comes to Kevin Bowman.

The walk isn't so far, but I half expect my dad to be sober by the time I get there, especially since I don't make an effort to rush. A sunset walk is something I hate to miss. The harsh heat on my back and the cool breeze hitting my face feels like being caught between heaven and hell. I find him sitting on a parking curb out front, looking defeated and irritable. Like approaching a feral dog, I walk toward him slowly but with confidence. He doesn't look up at me, even when he turns his can upside down, draining the last drops of liquid inside. I reach down into his shirt pocket, hoping to find money to pay for the beers he's had, and wishing money could fix the damages he causes. Cash can't fix broken souls.

He grabs the pocket with my hand in it. "Paid him, girl. Just get my keys."

I yank my hand back and walk inside. Frank is counting money from the drawer with both hands in a mad blur of green. He doesn't look as angry as he sounded on the phone.

"I'll take the keys." I put my hand out. "And thanks."

He doesn't smile as he drops them into my open palm, and I don't smile at him before I turn and leave.

I walk to the truck cab and get in the driver's side, starting the engine up with a mechanical roar. He's still sitting on that curb. I honk. Frank bangs a fist on the glass beside the register and points a finger to me—I must have scared him.

Dad gets up, finally, and gets in the other side of the cab, his body dragging behind him like a useless leg. He smashes the can in his palm before throwing it into the floor. "Don't tell your sister."

I look at him, my brows mash together in thought. "Why?"

"She's already so damn bitchy with me." It's slurred words coming out, and I'm barely able to understand them. I shift the truck into reverse and slam on the gas then the break, jarring his body around like a rag doll.

"Jesus!" He grabs the back of his head, and looks at me from the corner of his eyes. "Just drive, or can't you do that either?"

I pound the gas pedal to the floor and the tires scream, if they leave marks I'll be dead to Frank, but I don't stay long enough to find out. The town flies by, blending with the blackening sky in the background. I don't care if we end up wrapped around a telephone pole, I've had enough of how much he hates us. I glance at him from the corner of my eye and notice him staring, his jaw tight as he swallows then turns his gaze back to the road.

"You look just like her."

I stare ahead, unwilling to ask because I know exactly who he's talking about.

"You're stubborn like her. She was so stubborn, but optimistic too."

"I'm anything but optimistic…" I mutter.

"Stubborn girls." He muses.

I pass our house and the road takes us by the church, though I don't stop. Dad's head slumps as I slow our pace, and I'm hopeful he passes out. I glance out toward the giant church window. A spec in the glass or a shadow, I can't tell, until his face materializes in my sight. He's okay, and still in there. My insides flutter and travel up my throat in relief, and curiosity. I wonder why he didn't wake me, or how he didn't see me. The thoughts multiply until noises from the passenger seat jar my concentration.

"Where are we going?" He's slurring and leaning against the window with his arm. I really can't imagine how I'll be able to get him inside the house.

"Home."

I park in the driveway, instead of the yard, and regret it as soon as I'm halfway to the door with my six foot tall father leaning on me. He's barely able to walk, but I'm thankful for every step closer to the door. Each one gets us that much closer to this weight off my shoulders.

"Come on, Dad, just hold on to the rail while I…" I shuffle under his weight as he tries to lower himself to the ground. "You can't sit down, I'll never be able to get you back up."

"I'll sleep outside."

"Just…" I think for a second and bend at the waist. "Lean on me while I unlock the door."

He does, and I dig quickly inside my pocket for the key. I pretty much drag him the rest of the way. He hits his bed with enough force to make the blankets billow into the air like a parachute. I turn to leave, but he grabs my hand.

"What would I do without my girls?"

I don't answer. His eyes are closed and I don't believe he's sincere. He'd just drunk.

"My beautiful girls." He looks up at me and pulls me closer. I sit next to him on the bed and he pats the back of my hand with inebriated enthusiasm. "How would I ever make it to work? Or stay out of jail?"

His eyes droop and seesaw individually as his hand settles on mine. He looks like a wounded animal, a loyal companion abandoned by his only love, clinging to what he has left of her. Something in the way he smiles reminds me of being young, when we'd wait on the back step for him to come home from work. We would run around the back yard like there wasn't anything else in the world, only us and our father chasing us, telling us he'd get us and tickle us until we go crazy.

"I love you, baby Brenna." The whisper lingers in the air between us as I watch him drift into sleep.

I kiss his forehead. "I love you daddy."

The moon is nearly full and fills the back yard with a white dew, glistening off the grass and gravel. It's nearing three A.M. when I reach the church and my stomach fills with lava at the thought of going in, knowing what happened.

Unless it isn't true.

With everything turning out to be a hallucination, there's a much better chance that it wasn't real, but I still have no idea what really happened. I know he's in there, but what else is in there with him? My internal battle rages on when I hear a scream that shuts my brain down completely. All apprehension leaves me, and I'm scrambling up the balcony steps before I can breathe, focused only on the agonizing noises coming from above.

Niven is curled in a ball on a blanket spread out by the window, his hands covering his face, like he's being kicked by an invisible assailant. His cries are heart-breaking.

I rush to his side. "Niven." I shake him, but I'm making it worse, he just curls tighter into himself. I lay down beside him, slip my arms through his tangled limbs and pull him close. Slowly his arms relax, but then they jolt in surprise. We stare at each other for a few seconds as he registers who I am, and what I'm doing. It feels strange and intimate–our faces, merely inches apart–and he's trying to take it all in.

"Brenna?" His voice is strained and he's hesitant to move, possibly afraid I'll morph into the terrors living inside his head. A smile warms my face and I bury myself in his chest, hoping I scared away all of his demons. He wraps his arms around me and we lay there, our hearts slowly finding a matching rhythm, before he speaks.

"What are you doing here?"

I close my eyes, "This is where I've wanted to be all day. For two days, actually."

I feel his chin move, and imagine he's smiling.

"I thought they kidnapped you." He whispers with a kiss to my forehead.

"I thought I killed them. You didn't see me on the floor?"

He shifts, then cups my face in his hands. "I looked everywhere for you. After I gathered everything I could to throw at them."

He points to a pile of debris and broken beams that he collected while I was imagining a woman beast in the basement. "You weren't here."

My stomach turns in a tight corkscrew thinking of where I would have gone, why he wouldn't have seen me, and what made me come back after seeing what I did.

His arms tighten the slightest bit. "Will you stay here tonight?"

Of all the places I could be at this particular time, in his arms are definitely at the top of my preferred places list. I answer by snuggling as close as I can get, feeling the safest I've felt all night, even knowing a monster still might be a few feet away.

Even though it's great party early in the morning, I'm not

close to tired. I watch Niven's dark face in the clean white light from the window as he stares at the ceiling in thought. He must not be tired either.

"I haven't had any...visions...today." I whisper.

"That's good." His eyes momentarily flit in my direction, then he smiles as he looks to the ceiling again. My head fits perfectly in his shoulder, so well that I'm finally starting to doze. But when my nose fills with his memorable scent I'm determined to stay awake for as long as I can. Good things in my life don't last very long.

"Wyatt's ghost brother said the bone-crusher in the basement here killed him." I say, randomly, as I fade into sleep.

"Except that's an urban legend." He says.

The building settles; creaking with a horrible moan. My heart springs to life like I've been shocked with a defibrillator, and I cling to Niven with a childish force. He rubs my arm up and down from my elbow, and it's reassuring rather than demeaning. Comforting instead of patronizing.

"Do you go back to school in two weeks?" He asks.

"Senior year."

"Will you run away with me when we graduate?"

I wish I could say yes, but I hate the empty promises people make. I can't let him hope, just to crush him later on if it's not how things work out. It's not fair.

"I can't say."

"Why?"

I think of my Dad's face, his warm smile as he pats my

hand. "I have people."

"Who hurt you." He's seen my bruises.

"Who need me."

His focus above falters. He closes his eyes and whispers, "I need you."

My chest is tight from, thankfully, something other than fear of bodily harm—a fear of letting everyone around me down. It physically hurts and sours my stomach. I cringe as tears tickle the corners of my eyes. A sob vibrates through my chest.

"I'm sorry." He sits up, taking me with him, and holds my face in his hands. "I didn't mean to make you sad, I'm so sorry."

I shake my head, blowing off my overly emotional reaction, but a weepy gasp escapes and betrays me. He wipes the tears from my cheeks, his soft fingers exploring my skin, as I chance a look in his eyes—his shade of green has become my favorite color in the short time I've known him.

He leans in quickly and kisses me, apologetically. "I didn't mean to make you cry."

"I've had a bad few days, it's not your fault." We're close, our noses brushing as we tremble with shallow breaths. I'm afraid to move, I could break the moment if I do something stupid. Have I broken it now by thinking about it too much?

"Don't think about those days." He whispers and kisses me again. My stomach knots, paralyzing my arms that sit pathetically in my lap as I'm kissed by the best smelling creature

I've ever encountered. His hand tangles in my hair behind my head and the other pulls me toward him, suddenly, at the small of my back. It's the encouragement I need to let go of the endless stream of consciousness that incapacitates me. My arms wrap around his neck, and I snake a hand down the back of his shirt, but what I feel brings back the mind chatter.

A strange protrusion, like a broken bone healed all wrong.

He notices my absence in our kisses and pulls back, twitching away my hand. I look into his eyes, searching, but his gaze falls to my collarbone with a shake of his head. Instead of saying anything, he tastes my flesh from my shoulder up the side of my neck. Electrifying ripples of warmth spread in my veins, my eyelids falling in a weighted flutter as I lean into his mouth.

An echo of footsteps bounce off the walls and into my ears, but I'm not paying enough attention to care, only enough to register the sound. I'm floating like an addict during the initial rush of a high.

The basement's creaky door moans and panic pours into me, solidifying my limbs–the monster. Marks are surely forming on Niven's back where my nails are digging into him.

"Settling." He whispers, and meets my mouth with his again, but I'm too far gone.

"It's real—" I breathe, and he interrupts.

"Stop worrying so—" He starts to say something, but whips his head in the direction of the door to the basement hallway when a horrible sound, of something metal being dragged across something else metal, screams through the room.

My chest aches in anxiety pulling on my ribcage, imploding, like a black hole, sucking me into myself. I'm paralyzed again, but this time in cold white fear. Letting the air out of my lungs proves to be a terrible mistake quickly turning my inability to move into seizing gasps for oxygen.

"Brenna?" His soft voice is far away, and shrinking farther away, no matter how hard I focus on his face. He lays me down, but the blood doesn't recirculate fast enough. I black out.

CHAPTER TWENTY

I WAKE WITH heavy lids in bright, dawning morning light. A weight on my chest confuses me until I see a mop of black hair nestled right above my heart. He jolts upright when he feels me squirm, assessing my face, then smiles. I smile back.

"Morning."

I smile. "Morning" Then cringing at the memory of everything shrinking into blackness. "Did I black out last night?"

"Yeah, the church made all kinds of noises and your eyes rolled back into your head."

I rub my face as I sit up. "I think I need more sleep."

"How long can you stay?"

The days are a blur and I focus on what I did last to make things connect. Wyatt.

"I have to go, I promised Wyatt I'd go with him on some field trip."

He leans in slowly, making my head spin even more than

usual for this early in the morning. "Come back to me."

His kisses are drug like, draining my entire body of oxygen and muscle control.

I put a hand to his chest, "I have to go."

"I'll be here, waiting."

I brush my hands through my hair, trying to make it look like I haven't spent nights inside a dirty abandoned building, as I walk through a back yard toward Wyatt's house. He told me the pass code (our birthday), so I decide it's time to pay him back for all those surprise visits.

I'm at the edge of his house when I hear a window slide open, so I turn and peek around the corner. Curiosity has me in its hands, squeezing me tight and tightening the skin around my neck; I have a feeling someone is sneaking out his window. It doesn't matter if he has a secret girlfriend, I don't claim any hold on him, but I have to know who feels the need to escape unseen. Who would he need to hide from his mom? I can't imagine his mother caring about much of anything.

A pair of pink flip-flops poke out before the whole body launches off the sill onto the grass below the first story window. Blonde hair sails over her shoulder in a long wave of soft curls, and I see her face as she stands on tip toes to kiss Wyatt through the window. My lungs deflate as I slide to a squat at the edge of the house, the bricks scrape my hands, but I barely notice. It's Mabel.

I fall against the brick wall and drop my face into my

hands. I should have seen it coming. He was caught in her headlights from the second he met her, just like every other guy. Her ability to morph into whatever boys want, even when they don't know exactly what they like, is an unnatural talent. She must have fallen into a tub of radioactive spiders.

I want to run, forget whatever friendship I thought we had and hide from the both of them. It isn't worth it. They both use me and betray me, just like everyone else in my life. His dark rusty car sits in the driveway, the hood reflecting the mid-morning sun, and like a black hole it draws me in. I could wait him out and steal his keys, take it as far as I can, and dump it before I find something else to take me even farther from this hellish place I call home.

The house's side door opens and I'm startled out of my thoughts. Wyatt heaves a giant black bag of trash into the can beside the wall and catches my eye. He's shirtless, only wearing a pair of athletic shorts, and I grit my teeth, fending off the thoughts of why he's half naked and shooing my sister out his bedroom window. We stare for a long minute before I finally shrug, giving him a big, bug eyed expression.

"How long have you been out here?" He sounds guilty, but it could also just be my own skewed perspective.

"A minute." I hold his gaze, testing him.

He hesitates, then rubs the back of his neck. "Well, good. We can leave now."

I haven't asked where we're headed, and I'm not sure I care

anymore. The window is cold on my forehead from the over-active air-conditioning—Wyatt has been sweating since we left his house. Scenery screams by as he speeds up the interstate, north past Lexington and I'm officially the farthest from home I've ever been.

I focus on the blurs of beiges and greens, trying to strate-gically cut every interaction we've had from my brain. He's just another pawn that my sister will sacrifice for her overall game plan. I could never take anyone who falls for her serious-ly.

The landscape changes to spotty residential, then full blown commercial and suburban landscaping. We pass a water tower and miles of retail stores, snapping me out of my daze. "Where are we?"

"Almost to Cincinnati."

Cincinnati. It's a big enough city that I could get lost once we get to where ever we're going. He'd never find me. I could start over, and just blend into the crowd.

"Where are we going?" I ask, but he doesn't answer. A rock wall forms to one side of us and I search my brain for any mountain ranges that come this way, but it's only a short bit of gray before the road begins to slope downward toward a color-ful city. The skyline spreads out in front of a curvy river, all of which shimmer in the sun that's perched high above us. It's like coming up for air after jumping from a high diving board—a rush of freedom after claustrophobic feelings of death. A bridge rises up from the ground and arches across the river into the heart of the city, and I'm giddy with adventurous thoughts. The roads narrow and cross and bleed together before separating again. I roll down the window to hang out backwards, looking up at the skyscrapers that tower above us, sturdy and stationary on the ever rotating earth. A humid breeze tangles in my hair as a police cruiser slowly passes in the adjacent lane; the officer doesn't bother to look at me, but my heart sinks to the depths of my torso anyway.

"Get your head in here or it'll get chopped off by a truck."

I slump back into my seat. "Party pooper." I watch the white Impala shrink into the distance and briefly wonder if there's any way I can find out what happened to Danny and Nate. Is that something you can just ask some cop, and would they even know?

"Just looking out for you." He looks at me for a split second, and it feels like his next words are going to be, Baby Brenna. His smile is so much like Mabel's. As quickly as my good mood had surfaced it flees again. Back into whatever hole it likes to hide in. I wonder how long he's been seeing her behind my back. He spends all his time at the library, which would make it hard to have much of a life, especially since Mabel tends to work at night.

We drive around for a while, in what feels like circles, before he flips through some printed pages of directions. He yanks the wheel to the right at the last minute, flinging me across the car, colliding against his shoulder with a tiny squeal. I adjust my shirt and shorts as he slowly pulls into a parking lot. It's spotted with a handful of cars, and he pulls into a spot close to the edge.

"I'm not good with city driving." He puts the car in park. "The street signs are hard to see."

"At least they have most of them labeled, and the signs aren't in the ditch." I say, and we both laugh.

"You'd think someone would have put that Main and Summit sign back up after it was plowed into. What was that, like, eight months ago? Just lying there on the damn ground!"

I pull on the seat lever and throw myself back, my arm over my eyes. "Nine months. It was my dad who ran it over."

I expect silence, but the laughter that fills the car fills my heart too. It is a lot funnier than it is embarrassing, I guess. I remove my arm from my face and laugh along with him, until a rush of cold washes over me and I shiver. The shadow cast by the building beside us is terrifying, sharp and jagged like a medieval spear thrust into the air, and I throw myself across Wyatt to get a glimpse of the gigantic church we've come to. The bell tower is a silhouette against the blinding sun, and the thin windows that line the entire side of the brick structure are black, refusing to give away the secrets from inside; a haunting sight I won't soon forget.

"What are we doing here?" We stand at the giant doors, which very much resemble the ones I've passed by so many nights this summer, and he opens one, gesturing for me to go inside.

"I need to find Father Matthew. I found an article about the church and he used to work there." He's behind me as we enter the lobby area, there are boxy staircases on both sides and a set of spiral ones in the center of the room, leading up to the bell tower, I assume. I run a hand across the black iron noticing little notches and grooves I can't see in the dim lighting of the room. Wyatt nods towards another set of monstrous wooden doors and I follow him into the sanctuary.

The differences between a church in use, and one left to be devoured by nature are countless. For one, it smells better; not like rust or rot, but clean water and faint incense. Wyatt dips his fingers in a small pool at the base of a statue, and makes a cross on his body—head, chest, and shoulders. I watch him closely and hope to copy him precisely when it's my turn. He walks away, in search of his priest, and I stand in front of a marbled stone cut out that's attached to the wall. The ivory colored basin is an intricate scene of the crucifixion, his hands above him as he hangs lifelessly on a cross. I blink a few times, trying not to see the statue's eyes move, or the wound in his side spew blood, then dip my fingertips into the cold water mirroring the symbol Wyatt made.

Another difference is the detail of the beams and carvings. The ceiling is a bold clean white with contrasting wooden beams that meet in the middle, cresting at such a height that looking up makes me dizzy. This church is twice the size of Niven's. I smile at the floor; it's funny to think of it as his church.

My eyes follow the amazing colors and shimmering glass down from the ceiling to the back corner behind the lectern, things that collectively give the room its holy feel. Wyatt is talking to a man in black, whose white hair barely covers the back of his head—someone I can only guess is Father Matthew.

The incense, or possibly the massiveness of the roof line, makes my head spin so violently I search for a place to clear my mind. There is a confessional to the side of the pews, and I knock before opening the tiny door, squeezing inside the little room to calm my sudden onset of agoraphobia.

The tight space is comforting in the midst of my wild thoughts; I can't stop thinking about Mabel's hop from my only friend's bedroom window, or suppress the lingering feeling that I may be a murderer. I sigh and let my head fall against the wall.

"What's weighing on your heart?"

I gasp, "Oh god!" I wasn't expecting anyone to be waiting on the other side of the wall.

He chuckles, "God shouldn't be an extra weight, instead let him lighten your burden."

"I'm not even sure what my burdens are," I admit.

"Anything you want to say out loud, but you're afraid of being judged for?" He asks, his cheek visible through the fine mesh of the little window. His voice has a familiar tone, but the soft way he speaks makes me think it's a learned trait. Seem familiar and put people at ease to create an environment for sharing deep secrets.

I think of all the things I've been wanting to talk to Wyatt about, the things I want to ask my sister, but most of all, I think about how I want to confess that I may be a danger to people around me. I bite back the frustrated tears that gloss my eyes, and comb my hand through my hair.

"I don't know how to do this whole Catholic thing," I say, "Forgive me father for I have sinned?"

He laughs again, and it's reassuring. "It's okay if you aren't Catholic, you can say what's on your mind anyway. It can help you find clarity."

I hesitate. "Are you legally bound to report crimes, if say, I may have committed one but don't know it?"

He sobers, and puts his hands to his chin in thought. I only see his outline through the divider but I can tell he's torn about what to say next.

"I'm bound to keep your confidence unless you're planning to commit an act of violence." He says. "Then I'd feel the need to stop you."

I hurry to assure him I'm not planning a terrorist attack. "I'm just…" I can't even form full thoughts, the worries I've been storing in the back of my mind are spinning around in my head like a hurricane of guilt.

"I have been seeing things that aren't real. I can't tell what's really happening to me, or what I've imagined."

"Have you seen a doctor for your condition?"

I chew on my lips as I decide what to say next. My dad

isn't fond of paying medical bills, would be the most accurate.

"I'm not in a position to see a doctor. Especially about hallucinations." I shake my head imaging what my dad would say if I told him I needed a shrink. Probably something along the lines of, *you don't need some doctor giving you crazy pills, go get me a beer.*

He waits forever to reply, and I'm left with only my frantic thoughts as company. "Could it just be stress or something?" I ask.

"I'm not a doctor, so I can't give you medical advice." He begins. His words feel rehearsed until he leans closer to the mesh. "But from a spiritual point of view, you could be experiencing symptoms of demonic possession."

CHAPTER TWENTY-ONE

WYATT WALKS TOWARD me with a man following close behind. After the words, demonic possession, came from the confessional window, I lunged for the door whispering a quick, nice to meet you, on the way out. The last thing I want to hear is something may be residing inside my head controlling my behavior. I don't even know how people get rid of something like that. Definitely not drugs.

"Hey," he says as I stand and straighten my shirt. I extend my hand to Father William who shakes it briefly.

"Nice to meet you," I say, wondering if that's the common thing to do when you meet a priest.

"This is Brenna... Bowman." Wyatt adds after a second. "You may have known her dad, Kevin."

Father William exaggerates a head tilt in thought. "No, I don't think I do." He smiles, and turns to Wyatt. "It was nice meeting you, son, I'm sorry I couldn't be of more help."

The Father pats Wyatt lightly on the shoulder before he leaves us standing outside the confessional. Wyatt gives a shrug, and heads toward the exit.

We settle into a booth at a local burger place across the street, and I watch the shadows of clouds pass over the exterior of the church as Wyatt talks.

"He said he was there in the fifties, and he left before anything happened."

I graze on the fries in the basket between us, barely able to concentrate on his story, unwillingly thinking about being a spirit host. Someone who walks around like everyone else until the entity decides they want to act out some heinous fantasy, and takes over the body. The idea settles in my chest, and snakes through my veins—it would make so much sense. I've been blacking out more recently, and it all really started when I fell into the basement at that church. Didn't we read something about this during our first sessions of research? My eyes bulge from my skull when the memory surfaces. A demon that possesses humans, and alters their thoughts. The Pishacha.

"Are you listening?"

"Yes." I snap. "What do we do now?"

"Find the book."

"What book?" I ask.

He shakes his head. "I knew you weren't listening."

"What book, Wyatt?"

"Father William said there was a book another Priest kept

through his time at the church."

"What happened to that Priest?"

His face turns grim. "He went crazy and hung himself."

I choke on the water that had barely made it to my mouth. "What?"

"He just got all nuts, and they found him hanging in the woods."

I swallow hard. I have to find that book.

Our trip back to Hannigan is nearly as silent as the trip to Cincinnati had been. Once we reach his house it's already early evening, and something about going home gives me a defeated feeling.

"Where do we start looking for that book?"

"We'll deal with it tomorrow." He's acting dodgy, and doesn't invite me in the house, just leaves me in the driveway with a little wave.

I stand beside the car, shocked, and also slightly irritated at his rushed dismissal. I spent my day with him, and he deserts me in the muted summer sun, standing in the shadow of his funny little eighties bi-level. Tears fall onto my cheeks without my consent, in spite of the anger that radiates from my skin, and I kick his tire with the toe of my shoe. I kick it a few more times until the surge of emotions settles into a low hum on the surface of my body. A low angry growl escapes my throat, and I don't know how to handle the intensity of my feelings. It can't be natural. It has to be something hellish, something from another plane of reality. I wipe the tears from my face, and pull in a breath through my nose, making a loud sniffing noise.

A long line of trees and bushes edge the sidewalk beside me. Wyatt's small neighborhood backs up to a park that's overgrown and infested with bugs. Everyone prefers the sidewalk to the trail, myself included, but I'd rather not have to see anyone else today if I can help it.

The dirt is speckled with tufts of grass that are expanding their territory, and I have to push back a scratchy branch more than once as I make my way along the path. The noisy forest floor won't stop echoing in my ears when all I want is some silence. I try to imagine myself back in the city, with my head hanging out the window like a dog, the wind combing through my hair and enveloping my head in a tunnel of soft droning sounds. But my brain only shows me things I don't want to see.

Like the slouching figure in front of me.

It limps forward. Pulling a leg behind as it uses short trees for stability. Gasping slightly with each step. They're injured.

When it finally steps into a pocket of sunlight, I see it isn't injured.

Because he's dead. I watched Nate die.

I back away as he stumbles forward and falls to the leaves and dirt below. I can smell his decomposing body all the way in the back of my head. It fills my senses, reminding me of every second I spent staring at Mrs. Morgan's body. I run.

Before I have the chance to vomit, I run. Tearing through the impeding branches, and out to the sidewalk, stopping short of running someone over.

A lady gasps, and drops a paper bag of fruits that go rolling into the tall grass. Mrs. Peters is standing in front of me, shaken and elderly, so I quickly pick up her things and hand them back to her.

"I'm so sorry, I just—" I look back toward the woods, and there's no sign of the corpse. Unless it's still crawling through the knee deep weeds instead of walking. I shiver as I back away from the park.

"Brenna, sweetie, who was that man parked outside your house?"

I turn to check her expression. "What man?" If she has any idea how terrifying her question is, it doesn't show on her face.

"Some brown haired man in a little black car, do you know him?"

I shake my head, and start toward home. "Is dad home?"

"Oh." She clutches the bag to her chest. "Yes dear, he was outside screaming at little Hubert for barking earlier."

I look back at her, and nod as she starts on a rant about my dad being insensitive to her little dog's fear of airplanes, something she likes to remind us of when she doesn't feel like quieting her spoiled little fur ball.

I break into a run, my shoes slapping the sidewalk until I get to my street, then I skip to the other side and cut through backyards, keeping an eye out for a little black car. I hope it's only one of the muscled country boys back for their stolen goods, and secretly hope it's Nate, since he seemed the most reasonable, or maybe the least deranged. I walk farther down the street, no longer in the privacy of other's property, but can't find any strange cars or men. The street is empty, and when I stand in the middle, turning in circles, I get a strange feeling I'm being watched. Our road stretches straight and far, in front and behind me, but I can't see any cars or people lingering anywhere. I check windows, just in case it's a neighbor giving off the stalker vibe I'm getting, but I only have a light breeze for company. The trees rustle in the summer wind that chills my sunburned skin, making me grateful for the mild day.

I spin a little in the street, eye closed enjoying the breeze and the lack of scary things and people, until a car horn scares me out of it.

"Move it!" The red head girl, who just moved back home to the house at the end of the street, is being impatient in her beat up jeep, like she always is. I jog to my yard and watch her drive by, following her with my eyes until she disappears in the distance. She graduated the year before last, and had been second in her class, so I'm sure she received some kind of scholarships. Jealousy spikes when I think of how many options she probably has waiting for her, but it doesn't last long as I consider how I could manage a similar feat. I did finish junior year with a 3.9 GPA.

I turn to look at the house. I have to endure this for nearly another full year if I want opportunities like Jeep girl, if I want my pick of city to live. Only, the stomach churning feelings I have remind me of why I want to leave as soon as possible. Is it really worth all the pain and mental anguish?

The sun glimmers off the windows and reflects part of the road behind me. The path to someone who hasn't hurt me, someone who would run away with me if I asked, my absolute favorite prize.

I stumble on the gravel that leads to the church, the one I prefer to any of those pretty ones in the big city, and stop when I consider his words. Distraction.

Am I using him like people use me? As an easy way to escape my own life? Branches shuffle around by the tree line. Niven liked to draw out there, so I skip the window and head toward the noise, wondering what he's drawing today.

"Niven?" I call out, expecting him to pop out from behind me, or at least from a hidden place by the wall, but there's no answer. I follow the side of the church, and round the corner at the back where there are spots of dead grass mixed with waist deep weeds. The lot is a blend of dead grass, tall stalks of beige weeds, and overgrown shrubs. My shorts catch on a thorny bush that stretched its prickly arms out to get me, and when I try to pull at the fabric it doesn't budge. I yank hard but it doesn't tear, like I thought it would, and another branch scratches my leg as I wiggle the hem of my shorts to free myself. My heart is racing, and my face is warm and red, afraid Niven is watching me make an ass of myself fighting this shrubbery, when I hear the snap of a twig behind me. I whip my head around to find the source of the noise, but can't turn far enough to look thoroughly.

My shorts finally come free, and I jump backwards, away from the abusive bush, and search the woods for anything that may have been rustling in the overgrown vegetation.

"Hey." It's not Niven's voice. It's a man's voice, and a voice I don't recognize. It's behind me, and not too far away, I can tell by the footsteps crunching dead grass as he moves in. I turn to find a black shape, shadowed by the setting sun, that's closing in faster than I would expect of a non-threatening person. I panic, seeing Danny's face in the blackness, and take off running. He's behind me, keeping with my pace and calling to me, but I can't understand him. I can't feel my fingers or my toes. The numbness quickly spreads to my chest, and I stop running to catch my breath, but the curtains in my mind start closing. Squatting behind a row of bushes I put my head to my knees, trying to fight the oncoming black out. It doesn't help.

CHAPTER TWENTY-TWO

A BRIGHT LIGHT beside my head disorients me, so much that I can't see beyond my feet into the room. I'm no longer at the church. Sensations of being carried, along with aches from laying in the backseat of a car while it drove through our pot hole covered streets, flicker in the back of my mind. I can tell I'm in a hotel room now. The end table has a glass top covering the knotty wood, keeping it from being stained by cups and mugs, and it reflects the blinding bulb back into my eyes when I try to read the words trapped beneath the clear flat cage. Lucky Gun's Inn.

I'm at the hotel by the bar, and I have no memory of getting here, aside from those tiny tugging, possibly false, feelings of being in a car. The shock of it courses through my body, and I sprawl onto the floor as I reach for the phone. My hand grazes the receiver sending it flipping across the table as I fumble around trying to get a grip on it. I would look less silly fishing by hand, knee deep in a river.

"911, what's your emergency?"

"I'm in a room at Lucky's." I blurt out breathlessly. "I think I've been kidnapped."

I say think, because I haven't seen anyone else in the room. I haven't heard anyone in the bathroom. I just threw myself toward the phone on survival instinct alone. The quiet of the room turns eerie, like they've left me to myself so it would all sink in slowly. I may be in an elaborate replication of the interior of a room at Lucky's. Maybe this is part of some elaborate plan to make me hang myself with the phone cord.

"Mam, is there anyone there with you?"

"No!" I yell at her, exasperated that she would think I could call the police with my attacker sitting beside me. Like he's one of those laid back murderers who waits until the last minute to gut me.

"Mam, calm down." She is smacking gum through the phone, and I have to hold back the receiver, I imagine the blonde girl from McDonalds moonlighting as a dispatcher. "What room are you in?"

I set down the phone and lunge toward the door, but re-consider that idea. If he's standing outside smoking, or coming back from his car he'd find the phone off the hook. I hesitate too long, hearing the girl on the phone call for me to answer. "I…" I begin to tell her I don't know, but I do. It's labeled on the side of the phone. Room 22.

"Room 22. Send someone right now!"

"Just stay on the line with me until someone arrives."

I panic. "No! If he comes back he'll see me on the phone. I have to go."

I hang up.

I wring my hands, smashing my knuckles together until it hurts. The room is stiflingly hot, even hotter once I start pacing the room, and the air conditioning unit in the wall calls at me to turn it on. The dial looks broken so I don't bother testing if it's working, instead I peek out the curtains for anyone standing outside. Street lights illuminate the lot in bright rings, leaving shadows to crawl around the cars and gated pool area. There are three cars parked in front of the sidewalk, but none look familiar. Middle school boys grind there skateboards on the broken curbs as they pass around a cigarette, or a joint, I can't tell which from where I am. One of the boys hits the sidewalk hard and rolls across the ground, making me shift my gaze his way. Just behind him a man is using the pay phone, his back to me. He's leaning on the box, gripping the edge tightly, as well as the phone receiver.

The curtains sway when I let them go, making almost no sound as they flow back and forth in front of me. If whoever brought me here kidnapped me, they aren't too smart. Or they think I'm still passed out. Either way it's starting to seem off that I wasn't tied up.

I take the few minutes I have until the cops show up to search the room for anything identifying, anything that might tell me who has enough interest in me to bring me here after blacking out in the bushes at that church. The tiny area is bare. Nothing but a ruffled bedspread from my surprising attempt at using the phone.

Then I spot it. A thin book set lazily on the edge of the bathroom counter. I look back at the door before leaping over the bed, sliding into the bathroom as I grab the book and flip through it quickly. It's full of religious words, and symbols. I flip a few more pages and see what I was praying I wouldn't see, St. Dymphna. The journal Wyatt was talking about.

I have to read the book, if I manage to stay alive anyway, so I frantically look around for an air vent. I silently thank Veronica Mars for the tip, and the grocery store for selling TVs so I could watch those few episodes while my dad hogged the TV every night. The dime in my pocket is perfectly sized to loosen the screw in the return air vent outside the bathroom like a flathead screwdriver, then I pivot the grate and place the book inside. I drop the dime. I'm shaking while I trying to tighten the screws on the white metal back to the wall. It's so bad I can barely stand again to return to the main room.

I check outside, pulling back the curtain very slightly, and see the pay phone man has left. From the other side of the window I must look like a floating head, peering around to see if anyone is coming toward the room. There's nothing but the blare of sirens as a two cruisers pull in front of the room, paying no attention to white lines, or parking in general. My heart races, wondering if I should appear more shaken than I am. I suddenly fear I won't be taken seriously if I don't look like I'm drowning in a pool of terror. I back up into the corner and slide down the wall, hugging my knees and hiding my face.

They bang on the door before kicking the rickety piece of crap open, sending it sailing into the room where it hits the air conditioner. The machine roars to life, just a few minutes too late since I'll hopefully be leaving the room soon.

"Come out, police!" Officer Millard has his gun out, scanning the room and causing me to lose all connection with my vocal chords. A squeak, or a gasp could startle him, and my head would be modern art all over the wall behind me.

"Brenna?"

I shake my head as he comes to my side and takes me in his arms, holding me tighter than I really need.

"Brenna?" I hear the voice from the church yard. It's deep and familiar, but I can't place it. A man, tall with frown lines wrinkling his forehead, leaps into the room toward me. His floppy brown hair falls forward into his face when he's stopped by the other officer.

"Sir, I need you to step out of the room." Millard pushes me behind him, and places his hand on his gun.

"Brenna, are you okay?" He knows my name, and I know his face, it ricochets in the back of my mind without finding any connections. Something in his voice reminds me of my dad's, soft and strained at the same time.

"Uncle Wesley?"

Officer Millard asks me to stay put as he walks outside and talks to the man. He comes back within seconds with a license in his hand. Wesley Bowman, my dad's brother, my uncle.

"Looks to be a family dispute?" The short sidekick Millard brought along, asks.

"I blacked out." I grab for the couch I know is behind me, hoping I reach it before I pass out again. I haven't seen my uncle since before my mom left, before I could really explain what an Uncle was.

"I brought her here, I—" Wesley starts to say something else but stops, scratching the back of his neck, "I was at the gas station getting her some electrolytes." He holds up a plastic bag of supplies fit for the flu.

"I was just confused when I woke up. I'm so sorry officers." I'm embarrassed. Even though I'm not entirely comfortable being alone with someone I can only barely remember, it's overwhelming to have a person care enough to buy me sports drinks when I pass out. My heart just grew like the Grinch's.

After the officers leave, my uncle takes a seat beside me, placing his forearms on his legs, clasping his fingers together like a child preparing for bedtime prayers.

"I'm sorry I scared you at the church."

"It's okay." I pick at my fingernails, and chance looking him in the eyes. He doesn't look as much like my dad as I thought he would. "I've had a lot stranger things happening to me lately."

"I know." He says hauntingly. "You confessed to me."

"What are you talking about?" I ask, stunned.

He pulls out a stiff white fabric from his pocket and places it up to his neck. "Father Wesley."

I realize quickly that Wyatt introduced me to Father William right in front of the confessional. Did he come here to take me with him? Does he know what kind of a man my dad is? A surge of warmth fills my chest, wondering if priests can adopt their nieces, and if my dad would notice that I left. If he would miss me. I touch the back of my hand gently at the memory of last night. "So, you came all the way here to check on me?"

"Yes. And to find out more about your hallucinations." He pivots slightly toward me, waiting for everything I have to say. I'm so unfamiliar with undivided attention that I have a hard time putting full thoughts together.

"Okay." I start at the beginning and tell him about everything. The snakes in my hair, the swirling floor shadows, the spiders all over me, Mabel chanting in the bathtub, and the men being eaten. I avoid mentioning that the killing took place in the church, and completely avoid the topic of Niven, though I'm not sure why.

"When did all of this start?"

I shake my head. "That's the problem. I have no idea."

"Nothing stands out at all?"

When I saw that tail in the church basement, that's when it started. But I can't tell Uncle Wesley about that, since I'm not sure I saw anything. Before that, I could have sworn the neighbor's house was swarmed by uniformed military and exploded.

"I've been seeing things my whole life really." My head aches, and I massage the skin on my face with my palms, pressing the heels of my hands into my eyes when it doesn't help the pain dissolve.

"Maybe you should see a doctor." He sounds disappointed.

"I don't have any money."

"There are places that will help you anyway." He places a hand on my elbow and gives it a squeeze.

And put me on tons of drugs we can't afford. "I don't want to be tied to a corporation for the rest of my life…"

"If you have a real issue, you could be a danger to yourself if it gets worse. You need to see—"

I interrupt him. "What if it isn't clinical? What if it is something else, like you said."

He sets his shoulders, suddenly less of a relative and more a professional. "We could attempt an exorcism."

That cold finger of death slides all the way down my spine again, and I shiver in the spotty heat of the room, "I don't feel like I'm possessed, I just see things."

"You wouldn't necessarily feel possessed." He says and stands up, straightening his black button up shirt, and it feels like looking in a mirror. I do the same thing, religiously. I follow his lead as he heads to the bathroom, which is where I realize what he's looking for. I don't know if I want to admit to hiding it, or leave it to get later and look at alone. The conflicting thoughts battle it out inside my head like bucks fighting over territory; one pushes the other back, hooves digging trenches in the dirt, until the other gains traction to push back. Watching him frantically search the room for his lost book puts me in a trance, so the stupid look I'm sure I have on my face isn't forced, at all. I feel like the bucks impaled me, and I'm viewing some random person from a mount on the wall.

"I can't find it." He drops a phone book out of the table onto the floor beside him, snapping me out of my daze.

"Find what?" I ask.

His eye twitches a bit when he looks at me. "It was a journal, but I don't really need it. I was going to add to it." He walks to the door, and stops at the handle. "I have no idea what I'm doing. Do you trust me?"

I nod, but can't figure out why I would do that. Do I trust him? He slips out the door toward the parking lot. I barely know him. I wonder if he's coming back with torture devices to peel open my eyes as he makes me look at crosses, or if he'll make me bathe in holy water. But what options do I have?

He bursts back into the room with a rosary in one hand, and a Bible in the other, looking full of spirit expelling energy.

"I know you don't know what you're doing, but this can't really hurt me can it?"

His eyes flatten and he tilts his head. "No?" It's a really convincing confirmation of my safety.

He pushes me toward the bed, and tells me to lay flat and look at the ceiling. "I'm going to recite some scriptures, and say some prayers," he says.

The moments before he begins drag on like years. I stare at the textured ceiling of the hotel room, and find patterns in the bumps and grooves, imaging it's the rising and falling of the ocean from high above. Maybe I'm floating, flying above a salty ocean with nothing holding me down. Until something heavy sits directly on my chest, making it hard to breathe. I gasp and pant, looking to Uncle Wesley whose eyes are closed as he chants the same line from his open Bible. "As smoke is driven away, so drive them away; as wax melts before the fire..."

I don't hear the rest of what he says, because I slowly sink into the mattress, unable to move. The puffy cotton and elastic conform around me as my body creates a deep cavern, far away from my praying Uncle. Fingers, then full hands creep into the hollow after me, their long bones stretch their skin tight and translucent. A mixture of comfort and terror washes over me. I'm safe in a pit of softness, but being threatened by skeletal limbs. The inability to move pushes the fear from my mind to my heart, and closes off my throat, choking me on the dread caused by the pale hands descending on me. The room turns black above me as I hear my uncle, "May the lord be with thee..."

"And thy spirit."

I wake up in a church pew wondering how I made it there after blacking out. Not only am I seeing things, but I'm able to function unconsciously. Wonderful. I'm starting to think I am possessed. It's dark, aside from a white glow from the balcony, and I go toward it, without hesitation. The confidence I feel about it unnerves me.

"You're brave." It's not a voice, but the wind in my ears telling me what I am. I search for the origin of the words as I climb the stairs.

"And easily broken down into dust." This sounds almost tangible, but still out of reach, when I hit the top landing. I see Niven as I round the half wall of the ancient stairs.

He's dripping with blood.

Not dripping, but clothed in it. It fountains from his pores in a steady stream, and his green eyes beam through the coating of deep red. The blood reaches my feet, and he smiles at my discomfort.

"Are you okay?" The words come from my mouth, but they don't feel like I am speaking them.

"Better." He grins letting the liquid coat his teeth. I can't figure out where it's coming from, no person could hold this much blood.

"It's theirs." Like he can hear my thoughts he motions to the side where the two guys, Danny and Nate lie in a heap. Then he motions to the other side. "And theirs." It's my dad and sister. I reach to help, but I'm stuck in the blood that's pooled around my shoes.

"And it's yours."

"Niven, stop!" I scream, and the sound vibrates from my vocal chords this time. "Don't do this, please, don't do this. This isn't what you are."

I don't understand what I'm saying, what is he?

He's instantly inches from my face, still streaming thick red blood from every bit of him—it sticks in my nose when I breathe, and tastes like rust running down the back of my throat. His nose is beside mine, I search his eyes but they are as black as a starless night sky. When his mouth moves I can feel his warm breathe on my lips.

"This is exactly what I am. I'll bleed them dry, and grind their bones in my teeth."

Blood rivers flow through my fingers, and down my arms, as I run my hands across his jaw and into his hair. Something changes in his expression, but I don't know what to make of it—is he afraid of me?

I can't breathe, but I smash my mouth into his, reacting only on instinct and not on any of the thoughts in my head. Blood clogs my nose and veils my mouth as I kiss his cherry red lips. His face shifts underneath my hands, changing into something vile in front of me, black eyes expanding into hollows filled with writhing insects and a jaw that can unhinge far enough to devour my entire body. The creature from the basement.

CHAPTER TWENTY-THREE

I GASP AND cough, rolling and nearly falling completely out of bed. Wesley sits on the other bed, rocking back and forth like a child after seeing a car accident. Did I hurt myself, or someone else while I was dreaming? It was all a dream. I grip the bedspread beneath me, and the soft cotton is puffy in my fists helps me cling to reality.

He lunges toward me, onto his knees beside the bed, "Are you okay?"

"I think so."

His head falls to the comforter as he clutches my hand. "You just started seizing, and then stopped moving completely."

The fog in my head, from the wild dream of Niven, makes it hard to focus. I sit up and look at my hands. They're bluer than normal, like I wasn't getting enough oxygen to the places farthest from my heart.

"I was about to call an ambulance."

"What?" I'm glad he didn't. "I'm fine."

"Are you sure?"

"More than fine." I sit up, swinging my legs over the edge of the bed, and hop down to prove it. I kick a foot out, and give him a set of jazz hands just to boost his confidence in my stability.

"This is why I..." He shakes his head of something he'd like to forget. "I watched your mother with the two of you as babies, and I couldn't understand how calm she was with tiny frail things." He looks at his own hands like they break children, just by touching them.

"She must have been hiding some deep shit then, since she just skipped town and left us with him."

He studies me for a long time, long enough that I my face heats, and I wonder if he's trying to melt my brain with his piercing stare. I look away.

"You really believe your mother just abandoned you?"

"Well if she didn't abandon us, what did she do?" I turn on my heel, and throw myself into the fold out couch against the wall. If she didn't abandon us, if she didn't willfully leave our care to a drunk of a father, then she must have been kidnapped or murdered. I can't believe a decent person could have a valid reason for leaving their children. No matter how hard I try to find it, the sympathy I think I should be feeling isn't there.

"She died, Brenna."

The words settle on my heart slowly, as I process them in my head in a continuous loop. Questions start to sneak into the three word ticker running across my mind—why didn't he tell us, does Mabel know, and haven't I known all along? The fact that when he talked about her—if he ever talked about her—it was always in past tense, should have been a clue.

Wesley is holding his breath as I stare through his head. "You didn't know?"

I shake my head, unable to think clearly enough to chance speaking. I continue shaking my head as if it will erase the past few days like a picture on an Etch A Sketch, but all it does it make me dizzy. I'm sinking slowly in the flood of thoughts washing over my mind, suddenly aware that I'm related to a bunch of liars. No matter what I suspected before, I know now it's very true. All of them. Liars.

I snap out of my daze. "Why did you leave?"

He swallows hard, beaming doe eyes at me before they begin to glisten with tears. His hands collide with his face, wiping and pulling at his skin. A gesture that's vaguely familiar.

"I can't believe he's never told you anything."

"Told me what?" I get up, forcing myself to stay in control and not let the vile turning in my stomach interrupt this confession. The silence as Wesley rubs the side of his neck in hesitation is twitch inducing; chills snake through my spine and my mouth goes desert dry.

"Mabel's not his daughter. She's mine."

I can't breathe.

"I was seventeen. Her mother's name was Olivia and she died giving birth."

"Stop it."

"Your dad and Maria took her for me, but I couldn't handle it."

"What?" I ask, bitterly. "Not having to do anything? They took her for you."

"You don't understand."

But I do. I understand that urge to run when things hurt, when people hurt you. "What happened to my mother?"

"That's when I left." He lets his gaze fall to his hands. "She was going to get him from the bar and when she got out of the car…" He trailed off, gripping the hair at the back of his head. "Someone hit her, in the dark by the parking lot. Kevin hasn't let it go and I couldn't take care of him."

"You could have stayed to take care of us."

He shakes his head.

"He took in your daughter and you couldn't help him take care of his?" I'm angrier than I think I should be, and the violent shivering starts soon after I think about it. I shake, hugging myself tight, being electrocuted by rage.

He starts to say something, but I interrupt. "No, you don't get to say anything. He's been a drunk for my entire life, spending our money on liquid anti-depressants, slapping us when he was at his best but bruising us when he was at his worst and you were where?"

"I'm sorry." His shoulders are slumped in shame, but I feel nothing. I look around the room, anywhere but this person in front of me, who is so hideous to me. I don't know why, what difference does it make now, because he's Mabel's father and not just some distant uncle? My gaze falls on my shoes, the ones Mabel gave me, the only time I felt like she cared. I realize he's so disappointing because he's my future, if I give up on them. Alone and guilty for the people I leave behind. I can't keep hiding from them. And neither can he.

"You have to tell her."

"Sure." He nods. "You're right, I need to tell her."

"Now."

"Now?"

I nod. "And you have to talk to Dad."

He shakes his head at that, and gets up from the couch defensively. "I don't think I can do that."

"Why? He's your damn brother."

"We didn't get along."

I roll my eyes. "He liked you enough to adopt your daughter, I think that counts as getting along."

"I…" He stumbles on excuses as I turn toward the door.

"Take me home."

We stand outside Wesley's car at the edge of my driveway, while a cold breeze brings all the ghosts of his past swirling around us in a taunting chorus. I watch his face as he taps a rhythm on the hood of his shiny lease, waiting for him to say something, anything. He was quiet the whole trip over, and getting here hasn't made him any chattier, but it's not me he needs to make small talk with.

"Come on." I start toward the house but stop after only a step. Wesley steps backwards and places one hand on the car door.

"Brenna…" His face falls blank after being overly focused on the shutters, and I'm looking at a emotion mimicking robot who is tilting his head at me, condolence in his eyes. His fingers crawl toward the door handle as his eyebrows smash together, making his eyes small and the skin around them wrinkled. "I'm sorry, I just can't."

It's jarring, the sound of the door shutting, and I'm left standing in the driveway as his tires and the howling wind coat my tear stained face in dirt. Another gust of air cuts through my tee-shirt, and I breathe in the clean air of a passing rain storm. I don't need him. Mabel doesn't need him either.

I stomp up the steps and crash into the house, with a sudden audacity I've never felt. The door slams hard behind me, and I turn on my heels. There's nothing. No one, either. The confidence surging in my veins doesn't slow as I head to my room, the door is cracked when I reach it and when I push, it rubber-bands back toward me and shuts. The click of the knob is followed by shuffling, sliding, and a thud. The light shines between the floor and the bottom of the door, and I try again, turning the knob slowly in my hand, ready to use it as a shield for whatever may be lurking in the room.

When the light illuminates the scene, it's a bad sit-com in front of my eyes. Wyatt scrambling for his shirt, and Mabel fixing her hair back in a ponytail. I caught them in the middle of I don't even want to know what, but the knowledge hits me hard in the ribs, breaking one for each time I look at their guilty faces. The fact that they are seeing each other isn't making me giddy, but it's nothing compared to the eviscerating feeling their lies have on me. All they had to do was tell me. Liars. It's my room.

"Get out." I say it low and menacing—the only tone I have left in me.

"Brenna." I hate my name tonight, and the way people use it to try to calm me. I have every reason to feel the way I do.

"I said. Get. Out."

To my surprise, they don't fight it, just slink out of the room ashamed. They all betray me, why do I trust any of them. Related to me, friends with me, indebted to me, it won't ever matter. They'll all just toss me aside like an old doll. I may have cracks but I'm not broken. I'm also not stupid. Wesley was right to leave it all behind.

I turn to pack up everything I own and leave, whether Niven is ready or not. The image of the two of them together is burned into my mind, and I kick the door at them, knocking a frame loose from the wall; it hits the floor, shatters into pieces and floods the corner of the room in glittering shards. They reflect the purple of my shoes, and make my face bubbly and distorted when I lean down to sweep it away with my hands. There are dark pieces, bold dark brown spots like the painted lines that ripple under the clear blue of pool water. When I move the glass it's still there. The spot I noticed before is bigger, spreading like the house is bleeding internally from the corner of my room. It's at least as long as my arm. A face forms in the stain, a split second of someone staring at me before I close my eyes and shake my head removing all of what I just thought I saw.

I go to the kitchen to get the broom, but when I hear voices floating in from the back yard I stop to look out the window above the sink. Moonlight washes over the backyard, vacant of bodies. I open the door slowly to hear what they're saying but they've already left. Sounds of gravel shifting under foot fade into the distance. The door rattles with the force I use to shut it. The broom head is frayed and cluttered with dust that I try to shake off before I clean the glass off the floor. I stamp it as I walk down the hall and into my room.

The door slams shut behind me. Then the lights go out. Black thick nothing surrounds me, immediately chilling my bones in fear. I turn in a circle and search for the knob, but can't find it. The silence fills my ears, soaking into my brain like a virus. My heart beats an ever increasing rhythm after only seconds of flailing into the darkness, all the confidence I built up drains, spilling from my gaping mouth and bulging eyeballs.

"Where is the damn wall?" I scream into the void.

Something darker than the black around me moves out of reach, just beyond my arm's length. My feet won't move as I watch for the shadow to reappear, or the lights to miraculously turn back on. Fingers materialize, grabbing my forearm with force and when I recoil they only tighten, a burning and bruising force. I can't see my feet, but the bony hand, dripping rotten flesh onto the invisible floor, is perfectly visible as if it is its own light source. A hand from behind a curtain. I pull frantically, wishing I could shed off this layer of my skin, then fall to the ground, crawling away with the strength of only my slipping feet and one free arm. The creature forms in front of me, a man with skin pulled taut over his eyes, and blood lined teeth rotting and crooked, his nose cut off leaving only two fleshy holes staring me in the face. Scents of melting wax and lighter fluid confuse me as I fight my arm from his grasp.

"Leave me alone!" I swing my free hand at him, but it's useless. In the midst of my mindless defense tactics, I hit a sharp edge of something and I look down beside me at the glittering pieces I came to sweep up. Gripping the largest one in my hand I thrust it upward, hitting the melting skin of the monster hard in the chest. A deep groan escapes its decaying mouth as it falls beside me on the floor. When I release the shard of glass, light fills the room.

The body beside me isn't the monster I saw moments ago.

It's my dad, streaming blood down his side shading his bare ribs in bright red.

I stare, unable to move, then look at my hand covered in

blood from cutting my palm on the glass I impaled my father on.

"Daddy!" I say it over and over, pleading the words to fix his dying body. My hands instinctively go toward the thing invading his flesh, quivering above it hesitantly, and quickly rethink trying to rip it out. He moans and grips the side of my mattress in pain, closing his eyes and then opening them to look straight at me. I lunge at his face, fingers pressing into his sweaty skin, gripping his neck to pull him closer. "I'm sorry." I say it even more often than daddy.

"Not your fault." He pushes the words through his teeth. "Hospital."

I place his head back on the floor and rush to the kitchen for the phone, panting as I press the numbers to beg for help to save him.

"I need an ambulance."

"What's your name?" I've talked to this girl before.

"Brenna Bowman."

"Have you been kidnapped again, Brenna?"

I choke on the scream I nearly let out. "No."

"What's the situation now?" She's smacking her gum again, and I lose it.

"My dad is bleeding to death, you stupid bitch."

Her shock is obvious in the silence that follows my statement. "No need to call names, I need to relay this information to the ambulance, miss."

I immediately regret my outburst, but not enough to

apologize. Then it hits me. "I have to stop the bleeding."

Dr. Don said so, when I cut my hand, he said to stop the bleeding. I grab a clean towel from the counter and rush back to my room. He's still, and the sight gnaws at my insides that have already been wrung dry.

"Dad, you have to stay with me." I go to wrap the towel around the clear chunk but instead lean closer, examining the wound. The glass creates a screening of his layers of skin and muscle, and through the crimson streams I can see pales bubbles of tissues. I cover the pool of red in his chest, and the towel soaks it up, coating my hands in blotches of blood.

"Don't tell them you..." He whispers. "Tell them, I did this."

"Shh. It was all an accident." I beg him to lie still, but he tries to raise his head closer, for me to hear him clearer.

"Tell them I fell." A red droplet forms in the corner of his mouth. "I'm drunk, I fell."

"Daddy..." My chest rises with quivering gasps and falls, with the tears that drop to his shirt as I hold his head in my lap. "Stop talking."

"Promise."

"I promise."

I stare at this person I've known my whole life, and wish I had known the pain he felt, so I could help him with it. Who would he have been if Maria hadn't died?

It's a lifetime of waiting before the paramedics crash through our front door with cases of supplies and a stretcher.

Officer Millard is there, pulling me from the room into the depressing light of the kitchen.

"What happened?" I don't look at him.

"He fell. He's drunk." I say.

"On a shard of glass?"

I look at him through the film of salty water covering my eyes and blink. "I broke a picture frame." It comes out in a whine, pleading him to believe me.

"He just... fell... on it?"

I hiccup, and wipe the wet from my cheeks. "I was cleaning it up, it happened really fast."

"What happened really fast?" He's prodding for something, and I'm not sure what.

"The falling." I lower my gaze to the floor, I tell myself to make something up, and make it good. "I was trying to balance the biggest piece on my hand, and he came into my room in a drunken rage yelling about my sister, and I gripped the glass to keep it from falling..." I take a breath. "And he tripped on the edge of the door or something, fell right on my hand."

I show him the palm of my hand that's slashed open. It mirrors my cut from the nail in the wall.

"You're left handed?" He takes my hand to examine it.

"No." I snatch it back from him. "That's why it was a challenge."

He barely lets me finish my sentence. "See, we've had men breaking into your house to find you, you finding dead grandmas, and now you randomly had a piece of glass at just the right angle to impale your father..." As he speaks, they wheel my dad by in the stretcher, and I reach for him. Millard grabs my wrist but I shake him off.

"Dad, I..." He takes my hand and I walk with them, stopping to let them through the front door but quickly catching up by leaping off the stoop.

"Did I hurt your hand when I fell?" His voice is stronger as his squeezes my hand in his.

"I'm fine." I kiss the back of his hand and place a foot on bumper to climb into the ambulance.

"Brenna." Millard has a scowl, his eyebrows turning from two to one as they flatten across his forehead.

"Find my sister, Grant." Is all I say as climb in to ride along with my dad to the hospital.

CHAPTER TWENTY-FOUR

COLD FLOORS TRAVEL the length of the room, slipping under the revolving metal door that swings periodically in and out of the room I sit in. I watch it, barely blinking and never averting my eyes. Doctors and nurses walk in and out lacking an ounce of urgency, it fills my body with an all-encompassing rage. They don't care about anything going on here. Taking their time to get places, like people's lives aren't hanging in their hands.

The doctor said one hour.

My heart accelerates like a drum, getting steadily faster until it's thumping, beat after beat, streaming together like one long sound. Gasping and hyperventilating are my new friends, sitting next to me as I wait in a plastic chair molded for someone twice my size. Maybe I am small. Or maybe they're meant for couples. I realize I've sat down on a strange artistic side table and the cushioned wooden seat beside it is where I'm supposed to sit. My head slumps to my hands, my elbows holding us up by resting on my knees. I press my palms into my eyes and drag them down my face. It doesn't make the minute hand move any faster, no matter how many times I do it.

"Brenna?" The automatic doors slide open as she says my name, and she runs to my side, Wyatt trailing close behind.

I shake my head, bringing my knees to my chest and curling into a ball of heartache. I just want it all to leave me alone: the constant tug to one side, the piercing cut, and the deadly squeezing effects they all have on my heart. "Just leave me alone."

"We can't just leave you alone."

I didn't know I said it out loud, but since I did—"You all just hurt me, so why can't you go away?"

A hand squeezes my shoulder. Wyatt

"What happened?"

"Which part?" I ask, dripping sarcasm like the blood from under my bandaged hand.

"What do you mean?" Mabel asks, "The part where dad was stabbed with glass."

"What about the part where I was kidnapped by our uncle?" I hear my voice echo inside my fleshy cavern.

Mabel pats at my shoe. "When did Wesley come here?"

"When I confessed to murdering Danny and Nate." I'm tired of lying, and hiding.

"What are you talking about?" she screams, "Look at me!"

She shakes me violently until Wyatt pulls her off and makes her sit in the row of chairs opposite mine.

"What happened with your uncle?" His hair is tossed and sweaty, giving me too many unwanted images at once. I remember the book.

"He thinks I'm possessed and when he was out of the room I took his book, that book you were looking for, and hid it in the vent."

"Possessed by what? You're own crazy?" Mabel lunges for me, and I flinch even though she doesn't hit me. She takes my hands and kneels in front of me. "Stop lying to us."

I throw her hands off. "Lie to you?"

I'm too angry to consider what I say before I say it, it all comes out as a single stream of consciousness. "Like you lied to me about what those guys were looking for? Like Dad lied to us about mom, and about you? Maybe like you both lied to me about this?" I wave a hand at the two of them sitting side by side.

"We didn't—" I interrupt him.

"Don't."

Mabel starts to say something, but Wyatt cuts her off. "Where's the book?"

Mabel pinches his arm, and he smacks her away. "What do you mean dad lied about me?"

"Room 22 at the lodge." I admit to Wyatt and ignore Mabel's question.

"We need to—" Wyatt stops mid-sentence when we all

notice starchy blue cotton walking our way. The doctor is wide at the shoulders and his scrubs pile at his feet with extra fabric, his face seems grim for a doctor, though I'm not an expert in facial expressions for professionals.

"Kevin's family?" he asks. We all nod. "He's still in surgery, we're concerned the glass clipped the abdominal aorta."

I hug my knees tighter, and rest my chin on them as I stare at the doctor and his plastic sympathy face. Mabel invades my vision. "What about me?"

I hesitate. I don't want to tell her here, like this. She steps forward with a frightening expression, her facial features showing all the signs of being Wesley's offspring, and not my blood sister. My cousin. She's my cousin. Heat fills my chest and rises up my esophagus, coating it in nervous acid. Something wet hits my knee. I'm crying.

"You're Wesley's." I burst out unceremoniously. "We're cousins, not sisters."

"Shut up." She says it with a hard *sh*, just like I do. It comes through her teeth with a hiss of anger.

"He told me."

"Stop it!" She throws her arms into the air and walks away. She turns quickly, facing me. "You're just being a bitch because of Wyatt. My dad is dying on an operating table because of you, and all you can think about is hurting me because *he* likes me better." She points to Wyatt.

My feet are tingling from lack of blood flow, and when I drop them to the floor they buzz with the rush of circulation and anxiety. Wyatt walks away from the scene, down the hall toward, avoiding the confrontation. That small stream of tears has turned into rivers that drip from my chin. I didn't mean for it to come out like that, or at this particular time in our lives. Nothing seems to stay inside my head anymore, either coming right out my mouth as words or playing out in front of my eyes as reality.

"I wish I would have died in that ditch you left me in."

Her face doesn't change, or show anything other than the teeth grinding annoyance that's been in her eyes since she walked in the door. I wait for something, anything, but she finally looks away. My hope deflates and flattens to the floor—a popped balloon.

Far away. I have to get far, far away.

The hospital is a labyrinth of white halls and white doors. After I followed the paramedics inside, a nurse led me through locked side doors, and loud automatic doors, to a waiting room outside the surgery wing. Navigating the halls is frustrating, even with the abundance of signs telling me where to find certain types of doctors, none of them can tell me where I should be going. What I should do. I'm desperate to find a sign with instructions for my life—detailed ones.

My hand glides along the wall behind me, the walls are flat with speckles of dirt under the paint that tickle my fingers, but don't cut open my hands. A long counter that rounds into the lobby is stationed with a short, gray haired woman who is talking to a man in uniform. As I near the front doors I hear

Grant's familiar voice. "Not staying?"

I glare at him and turn toward the revolving door. I feel the suction after I'm enclosed inside, then I'm smacked in the face with humid air when I get to the other side.

"I didn't mean to be insensitive." He chasing me out the door. "Can I give you a ride home?"

I consider my options, coming to the conclusion that fourteen miles by foot at eleven at night isn't the best idea I've ever had, and that Millard can't be that bad of company. The storms have passed, but more are on the way. There is a sticky film from the air around me building on my arms as we reach the cruiser. I climb in the back and use the cloth seats to scrape it away. The cut itches under my bandage—a wound healing, but possibly leaving a scar. A scar to match the red puffy line on my right palm. One that may linger with pain long after it's healed.

"How's your dad?" The silence soothed me, but now his voice fills the car reminding me that I'm not alone.

"I don't know yet."

"But you're leaving?" He's pressing me again, for something I don't think I have to give. Unless I'm being paranoid. Maybe he's just a nice person.

"I need some stuff."

He nods and leaves it at that, and I'm thankful. The bars separating the undesirables from the enforcers is cold, even in the spotty heat of the car. It cools my throbbing head. My hand itches like crazy and I can't make it stop. The prickling sensation creeps up my arm and I scratch at my wrist without thinking twice. The invisible bugs nip and bite at my arms, then my cheek. I switch from digging a nail into the side of my nose to the side of my leg, back and forth until I feel like if I don't stop Millard will commit me. I don't want to give him any more ammunition. I place my hands together in my lap, leaning still against the partition as I watch him drive through the black back streets of Hannigan.

The tiny pinches rage against my self-control, ramping up their attacks and spreading to the back of my neck and elbows. A twitch develops in my upper lip.

"You alright back there?"

"Fine." I say it too quickly, but he just gives me one of his cowboy nods and takes a hand from the steering wheel. He reaches back, dipping down into his shirt to relieve an itch, something I'm trying so hard not to give into. Another one at his chin has him taking nails down the side of his jaw in long strokes. Something drops from his hand and I smash my nose against the bars to see what it was, but it's too dark in the black shadows from the front bench.

"Sorry my air conditioner isn't working too well today." His arm extends toward the dash to let him adjust the temperature, and something falls from his wrist. I pinch the bridge of my nose, knowing whatever I'm seeing definitely isn't real. His arms are dripping. When he pulls his hand back, after turning the dial, and goes to smooth his eyebrow. I watch as his fingers peel a layer from his face and see it fall to the seat below.

A choking sound escapes my mouth as another piece falls from his mouth—a chunk of his lip catches in the crook of his elbow as he drives, unaware. "Car sick?"

When he speaks, the melting flesh flaps around creating a wet echo inside the cab. "Yes." I take a deep breath, telling myself it's all in my head. He's not Mrs. Morgan. "I can walk the rest of the way."

"We're almost there." He says with a shrug. I guess he doesn't care if I vomit into the crevasses of his car seat, he doesn't ever get back here.

"No."

He slows the car and as his hands cross, one over the other. More flesh falls to his lap in wet chunks, and then the floor. He turns onto another less traveled road to let me out.

"You're that sick?"

When he turns to face me half the skin has fallen from his head, a cheek bone and teeth from a lip-less mouth stare back at me. My eyes shut, smashed together, and I try to blink them nonchalantly, but I can't make them open again.

"Very car sick." I murmur as I fall out the side door when he opens it for me. I stumble to a standing position, and force my feet to walk me to the ditch before I heave my guts onto the grass and gravel. The smell of under-digested food and hot acid fills the air around me, making me drain the rest of my stomach contents, until I'm gasping and moaning with nothing left to puke.

"No wonder you walk everywhere." He comes to stand

beside me, but I don't dare look up.

"I'm fine." I wipe my mouth on the back of my hand. "You can do whatever, I'm good."

"At least let me help you up." He says. I see his shadow from the streetlight shift, he moves closer, hand stretched out to help me stand. I watch from the corner of my eye, as a fleshless hand invades my vision expecting me to touch it. Blood and muscle glimmer in the light from above, and my eyes feel heavy again. I scramble backwards, wishing he'd just leave me alone. My legs, unable to gather traction on the gravel, make it impossible to not look like I'm trying to escape his help. My hand hits something wet, and warm. I pick it up and it's covered in vomit and dirt, with some grass clippings mixed in for fun. I gag.

"Oh." Millard steps backwards, not willing to help if I'm covered in my own bodily fluids.

I swallow the salt and spit collecting in my mouth, and shake my head. "I'm fine. I'm going home."

The front door is open. Mabel must not have come home before coming to the hospital. A sprinkle of rain hits me in the back, a tiny dripping cloud that passes over as quickly as it came. When I get inside I'm hit with an overwhelming emptiness, a feeling so strong it drains the marrow from my bones. I see his chair alone in the side of the room, sad and limp in the darkness, possibly never to be sat in again. What have I done?

The hall is dark, but I don't care. I walk through it to my room, but stop short. I can't go in there. I smell the blood from where I stand at the threshold, filling my nose with the sharp reminder that I may have killed my own father. Stabbed him through with a jagged shard of glass. Glass that cluttered the floor, made by my own careless, jealous actions. My eyes fill with tears, they overflow from my lids and rush down my cheeks. I have to leave before I hurt someone else.

CHAPTER TWENTY-FIVE

IT'S NEARING ONE in the morning by the time I pack all the things I think I'll need to last me on my own. I plan to hitch-hike west and not stop to look back. Niven has been in the back of my mind all day, but I can't bring him. I can't take the chance that I would hurt him more than his dad already does. I'd be risking his life, and I can't do it. He's better off without me.

Mist fills the streets with a sinister ambiance. Wind whistles through the trees and I hear drops of rain from the leaves hitting the pavement. It's a few miles to the highway, I can't focus on the exact distance with everything else in my head. Instead, I focus on the faded yellow lines in the center of the road, trying to keep in step with the edges to forget about all the things I'm running from, and knowing that I can't run from myself.

After a mile, I look up from my shoes and I'm not where I

expect to be. I'm at the church. My head flips in a circle around me, unable to fully grasp it, but I walked here without realizing. It's the opposite direction of the highway.

"You were leaving without me." The voice travels on the wind and passes me like a leaf floating on a breeze. My gaze follows the invisible words across the lawn, and my eyes land on a shadow standing by the front doors of the church. It slowly descends the steps, taking it's time, while I'm rooted in place on the rocky blacktop of the driveway. My heart pounds inside my chest as it comes closer. I beg for it to be my uncle again. Coming to his senses, wanting to be responsible for once.

His face materializes in the light from the hovering street lamp, casting shadows under his eyes and giving his skin a sickly yellow hue. "You were leaving without me. You can't leave without me."

He stops a few feet away as I shake my head in confusion. How does he know I was leaving?

"Niven." All I can manage to say is his name, and it comes out breathy and pathetic. I realize I have a backpack clinging to my back as well as a huge duffel bag hanging at my knees. He could see that I was leaving. But it really doesn't feel like he deduced that from my attire.

"You're in danger around me." I swallow hard. "I stabbed my dad tonight."

He pouts. "Is he okay now?"

I shrug.

"You can't leave without me." He voice doesn't have the same qualities I'm used to, it's more sterile and precise. Unemotional.

"I have to."

"Come inside." He turns and I follow without knowing why. I want to stop, but I can't. I'm on autopilot and it can't be switched off.

"Niven stop!" I yell, but he doesn't slow his pace as we reach the window and climb inside.

"Come along." I try to break away, but can't. I drop my bags at the window and follow him into the sanctuary.

I step inside and the air is so thick with dust that I choke, coughing and gasping on it as it invades my body. I grab my knees to stabilize myself. When I right myself he's gone, but the dreadful feeling his voice gave me lingers like an unwanted guest.

Sounds of shuffling shoes across the room catch my attention, the noise scratches at my brain giving me a terrible headache. Giggling echoes around me and bounces from the floor to the ceiling, right through me, but I don't see the creator.

"Brenna." A child's voice cuts through the air and I spin around, seeing only the tip of a shoe disappear up the stairs. I run toward them, looking up expectantly, but only see dust swirling in tiny tornadoes from being stirred around by a little pair of legs. I climb, avoiding slippery spots from the leaking roof, and round the edge of the balcony to find a dark trail leading to hunched shadow in the corner. As I walk toward the dark figure I catch whispering, and wet smacking sounds. Something strange reflects in the glass from the window. It's a little girl. I reach down to touch her shoulder, hesitating, what is she doing here? I crush my eyelids together, knowing it's all in my head—it's always in my head.

My hand grazes her shoulder, and the coarse fabric from her lacy dress startles me. Her head tilts backwards, inhumanly far, as she stares up at me with plate sized eyes, smiling with every tooth in her mouth. It's Reagan from the library, but she's different. Her skin is pale and unhealthy, like something drained the life from her. The air around me condenses as I take a closer look at what she's doing, huddled in the darkness of the balcony, alone. Where did Niven go?

She laughs and it stabs at my chest. Her head dips and terrible wet ripping noises fill the silence of the room. My knees hit the wood floor hard, and I grab her shoulder to turn her to face me. Reagan's mouth is dripping blood and flesh, her eyes are red and bleeding at the tear ducts. I grab her hand to find half of her forearm missing, white bone gleaming out from the remaining muscle and skin, shining like the way her teeth shine out from the chunks of her own body she has in her mouth.

I fall back, panting, "Reagan! Stop!"

"Why?" A piece of her arm falls from her mouth as she speaks. "You should try it."

I grab my head and curl into a ball, forcing the images of Reagan and Millard's decomposing bodies from my mind.

"Stop it!" I repeat the phrase as I beat my head into the floor, breaking the faulty wires in my brain.

"Get up." His voice fills the room. I put my hands over my ears to block it out, but it's in my head. "I said. Get. Up."

When I open my eyes I focus on the floor and the puddle of blood under me. I wipe my nose with the back of my hand, and smear blood across the length of my arm. Rubbing it just spreads the color, giving my skin a pink hue, and I can't stop the flow streaming from my face. It fills my hands as I stand. When I turn toward the stairs he's directly in front of me, smiling.

"Bloody nose?" He asks, taking my hands, examining the stains in my palms.

"What's going on?" I want so badly for him to not be a hallucination, but with every passing second I start to realize he may have been part of my growing delusions. All those nights I spent here, I'd spent alone.

He takes my hands and slides them across his face, painting his cheeks with my blood. My nose crinkles in disgust. "You're so beautiful when you're confused."

"What is wrong with you?"

"Lots of things." He smiles that inhumanly wide, clown mouth, smile. And disappears.

I shake my head and look at my hands, clean and free of any blood. I suddenly wish I could just drop dead, everything can go black and I won't have to deal with any of it anymore. No more family, no more hallucinations, no more blood and gore. Done with all of it.

I make it to the stairs, slipping slightly by the top step, and grab the half-wall as I balance myself again. My fingers graze a sketchbook—Niven's sketchbook. I ignore the curiosity coursing through me and put weight on the foot hovering above the top step. But the floor never comes. My foot screams through the air where a staircase was seconds before, and I barely catch the wall before I descend into a black abyss below. The edge of the wall crumbles under my grip as I claw my way back to solid ground, wheezing. The book is beside me when I sit up, staring at me like a sad puppy. I pick it up and flip it open.

The pages are familiar, drawings I saw when he first let me look through it, but after the hall of arms I come to an image I don't expect. It's of the break room at the library from my perspective, when I saw the shadows seep into the room and the spiders crawl up my paralyzed body. The only difference is a pair of eyes and a long fingered hand at the door, watching me from the darkness.

"How…" I breathe as I flip the page.

The next picture is of my bathtub. I quickly turn to the next drawing, unwilling to think about that night, and find an amazingly lifelike depiction of my backyard from the window above the sink. It's night, and the moon is lighting everything in the backyard, everything except the figure at the fence line. I turn the page. It's the scene from tonight, glass still in my hand, impaling my father with it. I slam the cover closed.

"You did this." I say. "You made me see all these things, you made me stab my dad!" I shake the sketch book in the air, and throw it to the floor in exhausting rage. "How? How did you do it?"

His breath on my ear sends a shiver down my spine for a much different reason than it did before tonight. "Do what?" Cold fear pools in my gut as he slips his arms around my middle, his cheek pressed against mine, and flips through the book that appeared in his hands from nothing. He goes through the pages, one by one. They're all blank.

Not a trace of graphite or rubber to be seen. "You can't see pictures that never existed."

The next second I'm staring at his empty palms. "Things that were just planted in your head."

His hands slide up my back and over my shoulders, down my arms to my fingers, but when I look down there's no one behind me, even when I can feel his fingers intertwined with my own. He is just another hallucination, Niven isn't here. I check for the stairs, and to my relief, they're back to where they were before

"I've really liked you, Brenna." His voice is the air, it's my own voice, it's all around me. "But if you aren't going to cooperate, I don't have much use for you."

"What would I do for you anyway? You're just my own bits of crazy." I can't believe I'm arguing with my own delusions as I back toward the stairs, toward escape. But I don't even know where I'll go to get away from it.

His laugh is reminiscent of the first day I met him—imagined him, whatever—except its louder, and frightening.

"I'd use you to bring me more food. Like you're sister and her lover." He's behind me again, breathing on my neck like he might bite it. Voices carry from the front lawn and I race to the window with my heart in my throat.

It's Mabel. And Wyatt.

I thrash my hands on the window trying desperately to convey how important it is that they leave, but it's having the opposite effect. They run to the door below, kicking at the solid wood panels, yelling reassuring things.

"No." I cry, mostly to myself, "Leave." I'm sobbing now, and I can't stop it. I'll kill them just like I killed Danny and Nate, just like I nearly killed my dad.

"You're not crazy, you know. Just easily persuaded." I feel a rush of emotions, varying from anger to elation, course through my entire body. "Your friends know exactly what I am."

"A demon?" The word floats out of my mouth and I don't want to believe it, it's so much easier to blame myself fully.

"I'm still deciding which of your emotions tastes the best, fear…" A giant black bird smashes into the window, right at my face, and I flinch as the loud bang resonates through me like a cymbal.

"Or lust…" The boyish face I've been seeing for weeks appears in front of me, piercing me with his understanding eyes, and the butterflies erupt inside my chest worse than ever before.

"That one's pretty good." The words slip out of Niven's mouth as he breathes on my cheekbone, trailing his lips down the side of my face.

I snap my head away from him but he appears just as easily on my other side smiling all the way into his eyes. I hold his gaze, trying to calm my mind by forcing favorite memories to the surface of my conciseness. Dad telling me he loved me, and Mabel holding me when I thought I was a murderer, and when I thought I was saving Niven from his own demons— when I thought I may have found someone I could love in a semi-normal capacity. His expression changes, just like a human's would, his eyes hinting at a flicker of surprise.

"Brenna!" Mabel calls to me from the hallway. They found the broken window, but I'm stuck staring at an illusion of a boy, wondering briefly if this person—minus the evil— exists or ever existed in a real way.

"I'll let you live." He says, only loud enough that I can hear him. Or he's saying it inside my head, I don't know. "You have to bring me more bodies."

I run to the stairs, slipping and sliding to a stop when I see they're gone again. I grab at the wall and throw myself toward the middle edge of the balcony, nearly flipping over the half wall, trying to find my sister below.

"Brenna?" Mabel calls for me, like I'm calling to her though I haven't said a word. Wyatt is looking through rows of pews, but Mabel goes straight for the door. The one to the basement. Breath catches in my throat and I know suddenly that I didn't kill those guys. It really was a monster. A bone crushing, man eating monster. A faint squeal drifts from the holes in the walls. Goosebumps form on my arms and I scream. I scream their names while I flail my arms. Her hands fall on the door handle, and she turns to Wyatt. "Help me open it!"

"Mabel don't open that door!"

She stops cold, "Did you hear that?"

"Whatever you do, don't open that door!"

She pulls her hands back and when Wyatt reaches for it she smacks him away. "Don't."

Her eyes search the room but she doesn't look up. I call to her, but she's focused on the corners and under piles of debris, thinking I'm hurt or stuck in need of saving. Footsteps slap the floor behind me, each sound snaps through my body like a lightning bolt.

"How do you make noise if you don't exist?" I breathe without looking back. The steps change to scraping. Nails drag and click across the surface like a tiger dragging a kicking antelope around behind me. "Stop it, Niven."

"I can make you think whatever I'd like, whatever makes you most useful. If I need you to run, I'll make you think something is chasing you." Warm fingers drag my sweaty hair across my neck and flip it forward over one shoulder. "I can make them think whatever I want." He rests his chin on the shoulder opposite where he swept my hair, and his presence solidifies my body in fear. I feel him smile at the basement door as Wyatt puts his hands to it again.

I scream, "Wyatt, stop!"

His foot slips. I hear Mabel's footsteps, but she's too far away, she won't make it before he finds his footing.

"Stop," I beg, holding tight to the wall. "Just let them leave, chase them away, please!"

"Shhhh...."

The door's weight is obvious in the strain on Wyatt's face. He's turning red and his arms shake as he pulls, but he's determined to get it open and I wonder what Niven made him see.

"Stop!" Mabel's at the door, pushing against Wyatt's opposing force, causing a plateau in movement. Something hits the door hard. With one look Mabel has Wyatt turned around, and pushing with all his might instead of pulling, like he was so adamant about doing seconds ago. They slip on the filth covered floor as another blow to the door bounces them like the inside of a sub-woofer. Something slips out the crack, a hand or claw, and I recognize it. Grey, taut flesh of the bone eater.

I can't feel my legs. My heart's pace has exceeded the speed where normal human beings bleed from their ears. And yet I still stand, staring as my loved ones fend off a monster, and I have one propped on my shoulder.

"Why would I want to live if you kill everyone I care about?"

He combs my hair with his fingers as I fret. "But they don't care about you." His voice is an attempt at being soothing, but he doesn't quite manage it.

"You don't either." I shrug his face away.

He grunts. "They lied to you."

"I don't care!" I yell at him but he's already gone, disappeared from the balcony to infiltrate their minds as they try desperately to keep the monster in the basement. I round the wall and close my eyes, refusing to let anything stand in the way of getting to them. The stairs may be there, or they might not. Either way, I'm going to the floor below.

The hard edges punch my legs and ribs as I slide down the entire flight blindly, arms above me to keep from losing control. The bruises will be worth saving them, if I can save them. I keep my eyes shut, squeezing them like a child pretending to sleep. I wish I was sleeping.

When I stand, one hand on the back of a pew, I mistakenly open my eyes.

The church's filthy, half-rotten floor turns black, spitting cold wind up at my face. Below me is nothing but the sensation of emptiness, making my head spin and my chin sag. I have to work at breathing, and even then it's shallow. I focus on getting air into my lungs, to stay conscious. The ground is bottomless, and there's a pit in my stomach nearly the same depth.

My legs slip, and dangle into the deep nothing below, flailing around where solid ground should be. I'm holding on by one hand, clinging to a floating bench, and nothing makes sense. I shut my eyes and swing, hoping to hit a solid surface, but I'm left hanging, a broken limb flopping around uselessly. I'm not even strong enough to save myself.

Wind gusts up from nowhere, sending my hair swirling around in wild cyclones, and I concentrate on the floor, on where it should be under my feet.

Someone screams.

"It has your friend's foot." He says it in my ear, like I'd enjoy a narration of Wyatt's demise.

Another yelp and my arms tense. I'm losing feeling in my fingertips and I can't hold on much longer. I know I can't possibly fall anywhere, but the sensation of nothing below me is debilitating. There's nothing left to do but let go. Let go of the fear and the guilt, and just be free.

My fingers stretch toward the sky and I feel the curve of the wood slip under my skin. I fall.

CHAPTER TWENTY-SIX

I DON'T FALL for long, in fact, I hit the floor as soon as my fingers leave the pew. I hit hard enough that my eyes spring open to see the ceiling and its dilapidated state, for the first time since I'd reveled in the massiveness it weeks ago. Something sharp strains the palm of my hand when I push myself from the floor—a key. The key I took from Mabel. I quickly put it in my pocket and scramble to my feet.

They've managed to keep the door from opening all the way, though Wyatt's ankle is being torn apart. He's pulling away from the clawed fingers, but every time he gets away it grabs him again, ripping flesh from the bone. I spring toward the door, no thoughts aside from smashing that hideous thing back into the darkness. The force I hit the door with is enough to injure it; an animalistic howl rings through the room.

"Get out!" The door cuts into my back as the creature tries to escape again, hitting the other side with immeasurable force. My feet slide across the floor, and I yell at Mabel and Wyatt again, telling them to leave.

"No." She's straining against the weight of the door and I catch her eyes, looking back into them with every ounce of pleading I have left. She shakes her head. At that same moment I stop seeing the church. The floor is white and the pressure against my back is lifted, leaving me sitting alone in clean, crisp air. I refuse to move an inch, knowing how likely it is that this is all in mind, and push backward a step just for the hell of it.

"Why are you trying to save them?" His shoes appear in the corner of my eye.

"Stop trying to eat them." I say as I lift my gaze to him, standing above me with his hands behind his back, such an inquisitive demonic spirit he is.

"If only that were possible," he says as he paces the area around me. His clothes are the same but his body is longer, and he towers over me when he comes to stand at my side. "If I don't eat, I don't thrive. You understand."

"You'll die in here." I idly threaten him, knowing I have nothing to use in my defense and even less to use to bring about his destruction.

"I doubt that, I'm already dead." He smirks, "Or I was never alive. I can't be sure."

A voice breaks through the pearly prison I'm sitting in, "What do we do?"

It's Mabel, and I don't know what to tell her. I grit my

teeth together, sending a throbbing pain through my jaw.

I scream, "I just want to set this whole fucking place on fire!"

Niven grabs my chin, forcing my eyes to look at him. "You'll burn in here with me."

I rip my face from his grasp. "I thought you were already dead." I smile deviously at him.

I can't see her but I know she's there, her arm brushes my temple as we press against the door. "Why won't this door close?"

The sanctuary comes back into view, flakes of wood from the cracking door float down in front of my face and land on my nose. "Part of the frame cracked and fell, it's blocking it at the top corner." Wyatt points above me and closes his eyes, the pain from his gashed ankle shows on his face.

"Mabel, do you have a lighter? Maybe this place is so old it will catch like gasoline."

I hear shuffling, the purse she carries around has an array of items ranging from dental floss to pencil sharpeners, and always a handful of lighters.

"Wyatt, find something to light and throw it in the door at the other end of the hall." I say.

"How do we know we won't just let it free by burning the place down?"

"Got a better idea? Like trying to out run it and its giant bone spiked tail?"

His face sours as he raises a hand to his own throat. His

fingers close around it, overlapping and slowly tightening. We're close enough I can hear him straining for breath.

"Wyatt!" There's nothing I can do if Niven's inside his head, showing him whatever he needs to show him to make him cut off his own air supply. Wyatt drops to his knees. The weight of the door becomes heavier, hard to control, as Mabel's shadow falls over me and she tears at Wyatt's hands, prying them off his own neck.

"I don't think he can get inside all of our heads at once, he's not strong enough." I say this mostly to myself as Mabel frantically pulls at Wyatt's fingers. I look up and he's turning blue, his eyes are bulging from his head as he gasps for air.

"Let go!" I scream and awkwardly kick him in the stomach. "Whatever you're seeing isn't real!"

He falls away from the door, leaving nothing between me and the edge. It buckles and an arm reaches around, gripping me with its claws. It tears the skin above my elbow in three long lines before Mabel throws her weight back at the door, palms flat hovering above me. Cries echo in the room, pricking at my ear drums like nails across a chalk board. I look up at Mabel. "Whatever you see, don't believe it."

"I got that." She rolls her eyes at me as we barely keep the door from swinging into the room. The creature on the other side isn't happy about being able to smell its dinner, and not being allowed to eat it. Wyatt is rubbing his neck, rolling his head around his shoulders in pain. He squats down with his hands over his ears.

"Make it stop!" He shakes his head. "Why won't it stop?"

I only hear the sounds of the thing trying to eat us, and when I look at Mabel I can tell that's all she's hearing too.

"Wyatt," I poke him with my tip of my toe to catch his attention. "Whatever you're hearing isn't real, and I'm one hundred percent positive this thing ate your brother. If you want closure you need to either help me hold the door or get a Goddamn lighter!"

He tries his best to focus as Mabel puts a lighter in his hand and points him to a chunk of wood, but the noise in his head is breaking him down, making the straight line he has to walk a dangerous climb up a mountain. We yell directions until he's halfway there, when the pounding on the door stops. There's not a sound from anywhere, not even the whistling wind from the holes in the roof. I slip to the floor and press my ear to the tiny crack between it and the bottom of the door, sounds of a wet mop hitting the ground and flipping back and forth grow quiet.

Wyatt's suddenly unhindered by the noise, enough to see the door he's heading for, and with a few good leaps he'll be there lighting that splintered stick and throwing it in for the monster to hopefully choke and die on. The whole idea of it sinks into me, and visions of him being snatched inside the room, defenseless, fills my insides with lava. In the silence I hear the scratching from the lighter, "Wyatt don't!"

"It won't catch anyway!" he replies.

I reach into Mabel's purse, hoping for another lighter as

she fumbles around to let me look. I find one and look for something to light. There's wood and dust but nothing to hold a fire, nothing to make something strong enough to throw into the hallway to burn the demon alive.

"Behind the podium thing," Mabel yells across the room, "They use oil for ceremonies, check for something we can light."

He limps toward the steps, falling up them and sprawling out of sight. Doors snap open and things tumble down in avalanches as he rummages for something we can use. The door starts buckling again, the strange clawed hands banging on it from the other side. Beside me, Mabel breathing accelerates and she drips sweat onto my face.

"Whatever it is—" I start to say, but she interrupts.

"It's not real."

Wyatt's head peeks out from the side with a giant bottle of golden liquid, "Smells like something that will light!"

Mabel's hands slip. She screams. I jump up and press my hands on hers, pinning them to the door. Our arms are intertwined, making it apparent that she's not just sweating, but trembling in spite of the strong expression she always has painted on her face. The pain in her eyes as she looks at me doesn't seem like it's caused by the door we're holding shut.

She searches my face, and I'm not sure what she's looking for. Or at. "I hurt you every time I try."

I shake my head, squeezing her hands under mine. "Shut up and focus on torching this shit."

Wyatt hobbles toward us carrying a jug with at least a gallon of holy oils. It's slippery, and he's struggling to keep it in his hands when it slides through his grasp. He falls toward a pew when his ankle refuses to hold him any longer. The glass jar shatters on impact.

"What was that?" Mabel's trying to see over her shoulder, but her vision isn't set inside the room—I can tell by the confusion that's creating lines across her forehead. I don't know what to tell her, to keep her from panicking like I'm on the verge of doing.

"It's fine." I say, my head bobbing slowly, like a trinket on the dashboard of a car. The bleeding on my arm is a slow trickle, the smell reaches my nose turning my stomach, but that's not what's making me most sick. The oil is spread out in a thin layer over two pews and on the kneelers below. Everywhere, and completely useless. In the minute light from outside, everything looks black and white.

"Will oily wood catch fire?" I ask, looking desperately at Wyatt as he stands stunned into silence at the glossy mess. I watch his eyes twitch. The door cracks under another blow from the monster, but holds. The only barrier we have. Hopefully it lasts long enough to figure something out.

Wyatt's expression changes as he stands with the help of the bench edge. "This fabric covering here might!"

The kneelers are covered in something torn and fluffy, plus now a bunch of oil too. It's the only chance we have to make something burn big enough to kill it. Crossing my fingers that fire will kill it.

"Can you break it so we can throw it in there?" I nod toward the door.

The sound of wood scraping across the floor answers my question. He snaps the dial of the lighter, holding it close to the fabric with his other hand acting as a shield. The lighter clicks a few times but nothing starts, no orange glow, nothing but shadows when a cloud hides the moon.

"It's not working."

"Keep trying."

"Be careful." I hear him, like he's standing next to me. Then I see him, watching over Wyatt as he tries to light the oil soaked fabric. "You shouldn't play with fire."

In slow motion the next scratch of the lighter catches a dry spot on the kneeler, and the oil accelerates the flames into a blazing line speeding out to both ends of the covered beam. It rises up high enough to engulf Wyatt's body and catch his cloths with it. He's burning bright orange and yellow, screaming in agony to the point I can't hold the door. I put my hands over my ears and turn, slamming my back against the wood panel to hold it with my body weight. The screams break though my flesh and bone, similar to what the fire is doing to him, searing layers and layers of skin off his body.

"Brenna, move!" I feel someone push me down, but can't stop the horrific cries from infiltrating my brain, tearing up my insides as I rip at my own head.

There's a long scraping noise that hits me right as the

screaming stops, followed by the slamming of the door. But when I look back toward my friend, he's twitching, black and contorted, next to the piece of the church he set ablaze. More screams fill the air around us but they aren't Wyatt's. They're from the creature. The echoing effect is unique, and terrifying.

"We have to leave, now! Get up!" Mabel is pulling me, begging me to leave but Wyatt is still lying a few steps away, charred flesh oozing out odors that make it hard to breathe. I can't be sure she's the one touching me. I can't be sure of anything if he's inside my head.

As if he knows my fears, another Mabel appears behind me, pulling on my other arm, pleading with me to stand and run. I can't tell by touch alone which one is the real one.

"Come on, this way." The newer one begs. I don't want to get up or leave, what if I'm the only one holding the door? Another voice is drifting on the air, one that I hope is Wyatt's, but it's too distorted to understand.

"Brenna, we have to go." The first Mabel says, kneeling in front of me and cupping my face. "It's not real."

"Now!" The other yells, and the urge to curl into a ball is heavy on my shoulders, weighting me down.

The first holds my face tight, squeezing my cheeks, "You have to come with me right now. It's not real. Follow me." Something in her eyes flickers, a reflection of a fire on the glossy surface.

I stand to follow her, but the other one yanks my arm hard. "Where are you going? We gotta get out of here."

"I can't!" I look from one to the other. "I can't decide."

The first one links our fingers. "I'm sorry I left you in that ditch, I'll never forgive myself."

I look at the other one and her confused expression makes the situation worse. The confused Mabel is the real Mabel, right?

"Say something, anything." I demand, staring her down waiting for the illusion to disperse.

"Thank you."

I narrow my eyes at her, puzzled.

"No matter what, you always try to save me. From Dad, from this, from myself…"

I feel heat at my back. Crackling sounds filter into the silence around me.

A loud crash startles the both of us and when I look for the first Mabel she's gone. The room is turned around and Wyatt stands, unburned, at the doorway toward freedom. I take a chance look over my shoulder and see flames touch the ceiling through the holes in the top of the wall. Mabel drags me across the room as I gape at the bright destruction of the place that's brought me nightmares unlike anything I've ever known, smiling at the knowledge that it will soon be ash and dust. Happy that my life will be normal again after what was starting to feel like the onset of a lifelong affliction, a mental defect to rival all the others I'm housing in this skull of mine. We reach the window and throw my bags out before we begin our exit. But not before I fill my mouth and spit on the floor.

Damn him to hell, or where-ever demons go.

One foot is outside the frame, ready for the second to join, when I see him at the open doorway.

"You said you'd take me with you."

His eyes are sad, but I know it's all been an act. Demons can act, right?

"I can't take anything dead with me. And you better leave me alone, whatever you are."

The sanctuary has caught fire, I can see the black smoke pooling into the hallway behind him, and I flip my other leg out the window ready to jump.

"But I need you." He appears beside me at the window sill, startling me so much I nearly fall out. Wyatt calls to me from below, offering to catch me, but I don't need him. I don't need Niven either... and how could he need me?

I look up at his face. "I don't need a self-aware disease." I jump.

CHAPTER TWENTY-SEVEN

THE FIRE CONSUMED the church until there was nothing left but some marble alters and an organ pipe, blackened and alone in the middle of ashy rubble. The police labeled it as a freak act of nature, it didn't help that the property owner needed the insurance money and Millard was looking for a promotion. Scratching backs in a small town: beneficial for all. They never found the creature, only the bones of humans said to be runaways, or hobos who died from lead poisoning found in the paint from the walls. But we know better, we saw it, and we have the scars to prove it.

The waiting room chairs are uncomfortable no matter what direction I lie in them, even with the pillow from my duffel it's still the worst I've ever slept. Wyatt is asleep beside me, that book from Uncle Wesley in his hand laying open in his lap. I take it slowly, hoping he stays asleep. After what happened last night he's entitled to a few days of unconsciousness.

We walked back from the church in silence, after Mabel told me they found the book and read it. The first part said there was a demon residing in the church, and they had a weird feeling that I'd been going there.

The book, written by a Father Joseph, talks in detail about their findings and the rituals they performed in an attempt to eradicate the spirit from the church. They tried to excise a possessed girl there, as well as form a large prayer circle around the building, to excise the demon from the entire property, but nothing seemed to work on the shape shifting monster that could look like a man just before it consumed a human whole.

Mabel stirs, her head on Wyatt's shoulder, clinging to his elbow filling me with warmth. Even after the lies and the history, it's nice to see something so normal. I flip to the next page, bored. Waiting on the ICU doctor is painful, body, mind, and soul.

The ritual Father William performed managed to do something, though we're not sure what the final product will be, we're still hopeful. His research on the Pishacha seemed promising, but this creature didn't respond to any of the offerings. We think our trials in rituals and prayer may have split the demon into two separate parts of itself, making it easier to destroy.

The last entry, by Father William, was of Father Joseph's terrible death by the jaws of the bone eater. Explicitly described, filling my mind with memories of Danny and Nate's deaths. I shut the book, tossing it to the table beside me and put my head between my knees. The world keeps spinning.

The phone rings at the desk and all I can see is the top of a woman's head, her hair wrapped into a tight bun, peeking out from behind the counter. She shakes her head, whispering, or at least it seems like whispering—maybe I just can't hear her. She peers over the edge before turning around in her chair to face away from the waiting room. I stand and walk toward the desk, silently, waiting for the words to clear, to mean something. When I'm close enough to understand her I can tell she's been whispering.

"But he's not flat lining anymore? Are they in the OR now? Should I…" She stops and whips her head around, gawking at me. I can hear the person on the other end of the line asking if she's still there.

It's not true. The sympathy in her eyes isn't for my loss; she's just sorry I've been waiting in an uncomfortable chair for the last twelve hours. This morning when we woke up to the news reporting about the church, a nurse had reassured us Dad was doing well, in spite of still being in the ICU. She let us look in through the glass window, his body full of tubes, while I stood with one hand on the cold surface wondering how I did that to him. How was it even possible for the big man, who could throw me across a room, to be brought down by a shard from a picture frame? I just can't imagine how it could get better, and then get worse.

I swipe her loose ID card from the desktop, my arm acting with my heart's instruction, and not my mind's. Before she can think about what's happening I scan her electronic key, and take off down the hall toward the room he had been in hours earlier. I narrowly miss colliding with a white coat and a few pairs of blue scrubs, taking no care to where my arms are in the midst of the hallway. The glass window appears when I round a corner, but there's no one inside.

"Hey!" Someone calls from down the hall, a rent-a-cop security guard who starts a slow jog toward me.

It's already done now, what's another trip down a restricted corridor? I swipe the card at two double wide doors, and duck inside before he can follow. He doesn't come though behind me as I run down the hall, and I assume his card has more limited access. There are tons of rooms this way, but I just need to find the one he's in. Thankfully tiny windows show the contents of each room, and most are as lively as a retirement home. Slow moving janitors or nurses setting up the tables. Or they are just completely empty. After a few windows I start to lose what little control I have, falling over a cart of supplies when I forgot to look where I'm going. Things fly off the top in opposing directions, fleeing to freedom around my feet, when I see it: a rushing of bodies on the other side of a window. The sounds of machines beeping, and people shouting, hit their peaks when I get my nose to the glass and then it all falls into dead silence when I spot the heart monitor. There's a line traveling ceaselessly across the screen; such a contradictory thing to do considering its meaning.

A doctor throws his gloves at the ground then spots me in

the window, holding my gaze as his expression tells me everything I need to know. Someone opens the door and I walk in, drawing looks of sympathy but unable to give them my attention. My eyes are locked on his motionless body that's already starting to fade of color and moisture, it's not him anymore. I lean down and kiss his forehead, like he did for me that night I took him home, and his skin is cold under my lips. He's gone.

I don't cry. Not because it isn't sad, or that I'm not upset, but because I don't know how. As the doctor leads me back into the waiting room I catch Mabel's eye and that's all she needs. Her faces crinkles and contorts as she tries to hold back the tears, but they leak out slowly in spite of her efforts. I sit down, back in the seat I've been sitting in for hours, and immediately feel numbness coating my body. Something that has nothing to do with the chair.

I flex my fingers, willing the blood to recirculate, wishing his blood would recirculate, but it won't. Conflicting thoughts fill my head, telling me to cry or telling me to move on. Both sound appealing but it's easier to do nothing, pretend nothing has happened and maybe it will all go back to normal eventually. Eventually.

Mabel takes my hand, squeezing. I look over at her tear stained face and swallow. At least we have each other.

Someone takes my other hand and I turn, expecting Wyatt in the chair beside me.

Except he's beside Mabel.

And there's no one sitting beside me.

ACKNOWLEDGMENTS

To be honest, I never imagined having to write an acknowledgments page of a book, because I didn't think I'd ever actually write a book. And now that it's done, I can't thank the below people enough for their confidence in my work.

My husband for all the nagging. I wouldn't have sat down to write if he didn't constantly point to the laptop and ask, "Are you working tonight?"

My sister, Nancy Pottinger, and my friends, Cara Harrison and Dara Ehrman, thanks for putting up with my constant book talk and never telling me to shut up.

Thanks to all of my family members for being even more excited about this book than I am.

Thanks to Amy Schardein, and Rebecca Cavey, for being the first people, other than myself, to read this book. I wasn't sure what to expect, but it definitely wasn't the enthusiasm they showed. Thanks so much for making me realize I'm not half-bad at this.

Thanks to Sarah Taylor for helping me make this book the best it could be.

To the UtopYA conference, where I met the most amazing people, and was given the tools to put my book out there for others to enjoy.

And thank YOU for taking a chance on my book, I hope you liked it, and I hope to write more very soon. Please consider reviewing it on your favorite website.

About the author

Amanda hated reading. That quickly changed when her sister started giving her young adult books. Since 2008, she's tried to make up for the tiny list of books she's read, constantly toting a new book in her purse everywhere she goes. She has accomplished reading more than seventy-five books, while being a mother, wife, and photographer, plus countless other titles she's picked up along the way. Her new found love of reading sparked her buried desire to imagine what it's like in someone else's shoes. As a result she's written her first novel, Harrow. Armed with a laptop, scrivener, and a glass of wine, she's determined to use every one of the fifteen plus ideas she's outlined for future books. If only sleep wasn't such a necessity. When she's not staying up all night, she spends her free time taking pictures of everything, watching a dozen different TV shows, and being distracted by the shiny internet.

You can connect with Amanda online at:
www.amandatroyer.com